SNOW'S ANGEL

SATAN'S LEGACY MC

ANDI RHODES

BLUE JOURNEY PUBLISHING

ALSO BY ANDI RHODES

Broken Rebel Brotherhood

Broken Souls

Broken Innocence

Broken Boundaries

Broken Rebel Brotherhood: Next Generation

Broken Hearts

Broken Wings

Broken Mind

Broken Loyalty

Bastards and Badges

Stark Revenge

Slade's Fall

Jett's Guard

Soulless Kings MC

Fender

Joker

Piston

Greaser

LAYOUT OF SATAN'S LEGACY MC COMPOUND

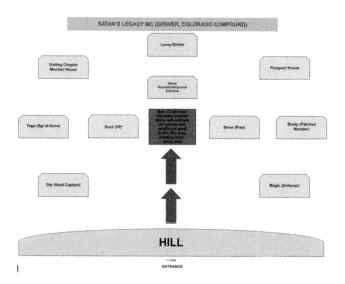

SATAN'S LEGACY MC

DENVER, CO CHAPTER

**What the patch binds together,
let no force tear apart.
Satan's Legacy now and forever.**

SAMI

"You can't be serious?"

Fear settles in my gut like a lead weight. It's two in the morning and Lennox is sound asleep, thank God. Corey is pacing, rage rolling off of him in waves.

"I want you both out," Corey shouts, loud enough to wake our son up.

"It's the middle of the night," I argue. "Where are we supposed to go?"

Corey advances on me and wraps his fingers around my throat and squeezes. "I don't give a fuck where you and the brat go. Go fucking die for all I care."

I claw at his hand and struggle to suck air into my lungs. This isn't the first rage of Corey's that I've been on the receiving end of. Hell, this isn't even the first time he's kicked us out. It is, however, the first time he's done it in the middle of the night.

A creaking noise reaches my ears and I let my eyes slide closed because I know what that means. Corey's black eyes shift from me to our son, who's standing in the hallway. He releases me but not without quickly squeezing against my windpipe one last time. I stumble back a few steps and take several deep breaths before turning to face Lennox.

"You're supposed to be in bed, baby," I scold, trying to sound like our world isn't crumbling.

"What are you guys fighting about this time?" Lennox asks.

I cringe at the way he makes it sound so normal. Like the fact that he just witnessed his father try to choke me out is an everyday occurrence.

"Nothing." I silently pray that he doesn't ask more questions or that Corey says anything about—

"You and your mom are leaving." So much for answered prayers. Corey stomps out of the room but makes sure to dig the knife in deeper. "You've got five minutes to get your shit and go."

The back door slamming rattles the walls, and I flinch at the finality of it. I rush to Lennox's side and try to wrap my arms around him, but he shrinks away from me.

"What did you do?" he asks with all the attitude of a seven-year-old boy with Corey Devlin's blood running through his veins.

"Nothing," I snap. "Hurry up and go put your shoes on."

I urge him toward his bedroom, but he digs in his heels. "I don't wanna leave."

I heave a sigh and swallow past the lump in my throat. Of course he'd want to stay with his dad. Corey is the fun parent. Sure, he's also an awful parent, but for some reason, that's not how Lennox sees him. Much to my dismay, Lennox idolizes his dad, and I'm terrified that he's going to end up just like him.

"I don't care what you want, Lennox." I use my harshest mom voice because right now, we need to go. There's no time for this argument. "Get your shoes."

"Fine," he huffs and stomps to his room.

I look toward the back door and see Corey pacing on the patio. I can see him holding the cordless phone to his ear, smiling as he talks. Two minutes ago he was ready to kill me and now he looks like he's happy as can be. I shake away the thought. It doesn't matter. He's dangerous and I'd do well to remember that.

I rush around the house to grab up anything I can, anything that will fit in the small duffel bag I have. It's the same bag I left home with at sixteen, the one I shoved in the back seat of Corey's rusted out Chevy. I was pregnant and full of rebellion because my parents wanted me to abort our baby. I don't regret my decision to have my son. But I do regret thinking I needed to be with his dad because of it.

"I'm ready."

I whirl around and see a sullen Lennox standing behind me, tattered second-hand Nike's on his feet and a ratty old teddy bear that he's had since he was born. I try to reconcile the little boy holding a stuffed animal with the boy that is so much like his dad. I remind myself that somewhere in Lennox is my DNA, and without Corey's influence, maybe he'll change. God help me if he doesn't.

I lift the royal blue winter coat off the couch and thrust it at him. "Here, put this on."

"I don't need no jacket."

"It's December in Colorado and it's cold out."

"I'm not wearing a damn jacket." Lennox crosses his arms over his chest, his teddy bear squished against his tiny body.

I drop my head and take a few deep breaths to steady myself. *He's acting out, Sami. Once we're away from Corey, he'll be better.* I repeat that in my head, over and over again, until I convince myself that I believe it.

"Put the coat on. Now."

Apparently, the harshness in my tone is enough to make him second-guess if this is an argument he wants to continue. He yanks the jacket out of my hands and does as he's told. While he's doing that, I search the room for my own coat and come up empty. Damn, where did I leave it?

I jump at the unmistakable sound of the back door creaking open. Forgetting my own warning to Lennox about the cold, I sling the duffel bag over my shoulder and grab my son's hand to drag him out the front door into the frigid Colorado winter temperatures.

Neither of us say a word as we trudge down the street, past the rundown houses of our neighbors. I don't let myself look back until we reach the corner. Just before we turn right, I glance behind me. My shoulders sag when I see that our front yard is empty. Silly me thought that maybe, just maybe, Corey would regret kicking us out and coming running after us.

It's better this way, Sami. You're free. You and Lennox are freezing, but you're free.

"Where are we going?"

Lennox's teeth chatter as he speaks. I don't allow myself to stop walking and answer him until we've gotten down another block. When I do stop, I crouch down and look into my son's blue eyes. I've never lied to my son, and I don't intend to start now.

"I don't know."

I rub my hands up and down his arms, trying like hell to warm him up as best I can. I ignore the tingling in my own body. I've been out in the cold before, although I was the kid in that situation and not the parent.

"I don't know why I had to come," Lennox whines. "Dad woulda let me stay."

I clench my jaw, forcing the words that are on the tip of my tongue to stay where they are. I grew up with parents who hated each other, and I promised myself I wouldn't act

4

like them with my own son. An idea hits me, and I smile as widely as my shivering will allow.

"Why don't we treat this like an adventure?"

"Mom." Lennox drags the word out dramatically.

As my plan solidifies in my brain, I reach for my purse, which is usually slung over my shoulder when I'm not at home and am met with nothing.

"Dammit!"

"What?" Lennox narrows his eyes.

"Nothing, baby."

I think back over everything that happened when I got home from work at the diner. I walked inside and Corey had immediately started yelling at me. I remember being tired and wanting to do nothing but get off of my feet after a long day but that wasn't going to happen once he got into his tirade. It was the same old shit. I'm never home, he's always gotta take care of 'the brat', he needed money for a fix and—

Shit! He yanked my purse off of my shoulder to rifle through it for money. And I bet it's on the floor, right where he tossed it after he stole my thirty-six dollars in tips.

I glance at my son and paste a smile on my face. It's going to be okay. Everything is going to be just fine. We have no money, no place to go, and it's frigid outside. But we're good.

I tip my head back and stare at the sky, silently praying for whoever or whatever is up there to throw me a bone, give me a sign as to what I'm supposed to do to fix this. After a few seconds, something wet hits my cheek and I know that was the higher power's way of flipping me the bird.

Big, fat snowflakes cascade out of the black expanse above us. I grab Lennox's hand and pull him along with me as I continue to walk farther from our home.

After trudging through the cold for a few miles, we're closer to downtown, and while the thought of the city in the middle of the night is scary, it's our only option. Maybe we'll get lucky and the shelter on Third street will let us in.

The longer we walk, the slower our steps become. I finally see the sign for the shelter ahead, and relief washes over me. My fingers and toes are numb, my legs burn, and my vision is starting to blur. I want to stop, to lie down right where I am, but the small hand in mine is what keeps me going.

When we reach the door, I try to lift my arm to knock, as the sign posted on the wood instructs, but it's impossible.

"B-b-baby, go a-ahead."

I struggle to form words as my teeth chatter but am grateful when my son's hand leaves mine. Before his fist connects with the wooden barrier that separates us from warmth, I give in to the unrelenting cold. I feel myself fall. I feel the wet snow seep through the fabric of my clothes. I feel everything as if it's happening in slow motion and I'm powerless to stop it.

At least I can die knowing I got my baby to safety.

SNOW

"You know you can leave, right?"

I twist in my chair to look at Heather. She's exactly my type and I've debated on trying to seduce her into my bed many times but always stop short of actually hitting on her. She's just not the kind of woman I can take back to the club to fuck and forget. Not to mention, I have to see her on a pretty regular basis since Satan's Legacy MC partners with the shelter to provide protection.

Never shit where you eat. That's my motto. Or at least, it's one of many.

"We do this every time I'm here, Heather," I remind her with a smile in my tone. "I'll leave when the sun comes up."

I rise from my chair and walk to the window. I heard it was supposed to snow tonight, but the weatherman is an idiot. He said less than an inch and in the last half hour we've already surpassed that and there's no indication that it's going to slow down any time soon.

Heather appears by my side and crosses her arms over her chest. It takes all of my willpower not to glance down and enjoy the way it pushes her tits up and almost causes them to spill out over her low-cut top. Heather is great at her job, but she has no clue how to dress for it.

"It's really coming down out there," she observes. She shifts and rests her hand on my forearm. "You're not gonna be able to ride home in this. I can drive you when my shift's over."

I stare at where she's touching me. My skin tingles under her touch, but the rest of me just feels itchy because of it. I don't like to be touched unless I invite it, and even a woman who I have no doubt would be a good fuck isn't immune to those feelings.

"I'll just have Duck pick me up." I pull away from her and instantly feel better. "I'm gonna do my rounds."

I stroll through the building, checking on all the people sleeping on cots. I make my way through the offices of the shelter, flipping lights on and off as I do so I can be sure there's no evil lurking in the shadows. This is why Satan's Legacy is here, after all. Well, that, and to make sure that nothing goes wrong with the homeless that utilize the shelter.

Our partnership started when a man showed up one night and caused a scene. Between his yelling and throwing things, he made such a ruckus that I, along with a few of the brothers, heard him while we were waiting for the light to turn green in front of the shelter.

There was no thinking, just pure reaction. We burst through the door in time to stop him from throwing a chair at one of the workers. We made it a point to stop in every night after that. That was two years ago. At the time, I wouldn't have guessed we'd still be providing protection, but it turns out that it's great press for the club and we all feel good about it. Being one percenters means we'll take the win wherever we can get it.

Shaking my head clear of my thoughts, I reach the last

thing I check every time I do my rounds. I assure myself that the front door is locked, and as I turn away to head back to the same chair I park my ass in every time I'm here, a faint banging reaches my ears. I stop in my tracks to listen for the noise again but it's silent.

A few more steps and I hear it again, only this time it's accompanied by a voice demanding to be let in. I rush back to the door and flip the lock so I can yank it open.

"You gotta let us in!"

A little boy, no more than six or seven barrels in out of the cold and my focus on him is so intense that it takes a minute for his words to register.

"Us?"

The boy is frantic, but his words aren't making any sense. I catch 'kicked out', 'bitch', 'dad' and a few others, but that's it. I look beyond him to the doorway, hoping to see an adult standing there, but that's not the sight that greets me.

There, on the cold ground in the doorway, is a woman. I rush forward and stoop down to get a better look. I feel for a pulse and my muscles relax slightly when a thump hits my fingertips. It's faint, but it's there. I scoop her up in my arms and kick the door shut behind me.

"Hey kid. Lock the door." I watch as he does as I ask and returns to my side. "What's your name?"

"Lennox," he responds.

His eyes roam over me, and I tense up as I wait for the fear that usually comes from little kids. I know I can be intimidating at six foot four and covered in tattoos. The white skull with devil horns on my cut never helps that image either. Usually, I crave the fear when people realize who I am, but it's different with kids.

"Hi Lennox." I shift the woman in my arms and start walking toward the shower room. "I'm Zeke. My friends call me Snow, though."

"I'm not your friend," he says as he follows on my heels. His attitude surprises me because it seems to appear out of nowhere. "Can you help my mom?"

"I'm gonna try." I look at the woman's face and cringe when I see the blue tint to her lips. "Can you tell me what happened?"

I carry her through the main room and catch sight of Heather rushing toward us. Her eyes are wide with concern, but when her gaze lands on Lennox, she schools her features. When she reaches my side, she places her hand on the woman's forehead.

"She's freezing," she exclaims.

"No shit." I slam my mouth shut and shoot a quick glance in Lennox's direction. He doesn't appear phased by my word choice, so I shrug it off. "I'm gonna put her in a hot bath and see if I can get her body temp up."

"Okay." She focuses on Lennox. "Why don't you come with me, and I'll get you something to eat?"

Lennox's eyes dart back and forth between us, and I breathe a sigh of relief when he decides to go with Heather. I would have been okay with it if he chose to stay with his mom, but this will let me focus on the task of getting her warm.

I gently lay her down on the floor so I can get the water going. When there's enough in the tub that I'm confident her body will be submerged, I methodically strip her wet clothes off of her. I can't help but notice her curves and I mentally chastise myself for it.

"I don't know if you can hear me," I whisper to her as I lift her off the floor to put her in the tub. "But you're safe now."

The water distorts her features but it's impossible to ignore that she's perfectly built. Small, curves for days, tits that are perfect to bury my head in. There are a few scars on her stomach, but they're barely noticeable.

I continue to monitor the water temperature, and each time it cools, I turn on the tap and add more hot water. I have no idea how long it takes, but her skin is regaining color and the blue tint fades. She stirs and seems to come alive in a flurry of flailing arms and legs.

Her head swivels, presumably to take in her surroundings. When she lunges to her feet, I instinctively reach out to keep her from falling. My hands land on her waist and a jolt of electricity zings through me at the contact.

For her, I don't think it's quite the same. She smacks my hands away and opens her mouth. The scream that tears out of her is so shocking that I'm stunned to the point of not seeing the fist she swings at my face.

SAMI

"*W*hat the fuck, lady?"

The man doesn't seem hurt by my punch, but he's surprised enough that I can step over the ledge of the tub. I don't make it far before he grips my shoulders and holds me in place. I open my mouth to scream again, and his hand covers it.

"You're gonna wake everyone if you keep that shit up," he growls. I try to speak but can't. "Are you gonna scream?"

Hell yes, I'm going to scream.

I shake my head from side to side, hoping he believes my silent answer. He slowly pulls his hand away, and the second my mouth starts to widen, he puts it back.

"Look, lady. I don't like this any more than you do." An involuntary shudder wracks my body. He arches a brow. "I'm gonna drop my hand again, but for the love of God, don't scream."

Our eyes lock and somehow, despite my very nude, cold, scared state, I see something in his gaze that tells me that maybe, just maybe, I can trust him. I nod. He releases me and takes a step back with his hands raised in a gesture of surrender.

I open my mouth again, but he reaches out toward me, and I slam it shut.

"Good," he says and drops his hands to his sides. "Do you know where you are?"

I think about his question and answer with one of my own. "Where are my clothes?"

He nods toward the floor. I follow his gaze and see my clothes crumpled on the floor. I bend down to snatch them up and dread weighs me down when I feel how wet and cold they are. All my bravado leaves me, and I fall back on my ass. Tears burn the back of my eyes, and I can't stop them from spilling over.

The man kneels next to me and something fluffy is wrapped around my shoulders. It registers that it's a towel, and I grip the corners to cover as much of me as possible.

"I'll be right back."

The man stands and his boots echo across the tile floor as he leaves me alone. The events of the evening slowly start to creep back in, and my crying immediately stops as panic snaps into place.

"Lennox," I say on a heavy breath.

I lunge to my feet and run in the direction the man did. I see him turn left and follow him, ignoring the fact that all I have covering me is a plush towel. Before I reach the spot where he turned, he steps back into view with a blanket draped over his arm.

"Where's my son?" I demand as I close the distance between us. "Lennox. Where's Lennox?"

The man doesn't answer until he's wrapped the blanket around me. While I'm grateful to be covered up and warm, I can't relax. Not even a little bit.

"I asked you a—"

"He's with Heather. She was going to try to find him something to eat." His voice is gravelly and reminds me of Tom at the diner. Tom smokes a pack of Marlboro Reds every day, and anyone who hears him speak could figure that out.

"Who the hell is Heather?"

"She's one of the staff here at the shelter." He thrusts a hand through his unruly hair. "C'mon. I'll take you to him."

I flinch away when he tries to put his arm around me to guide me in the direction he wants to go. He heaves a sigh and shoves his hands into his pockets. He walks in front of me, and I fix my stare on the patch on his leather vest. A devil-horned skull stares back at me. I ignore it and read the words on the other patches above and below it.

One reads 'Satan's Legacy MC' while another reads 'President'. There's a third patch that says 'Denver, CO Chapter'. I've heard of Satan's Legacy. They're a bunch of bikers who do illegal shit. They come into the diner sometimes, but I always pass off their table to one of the other waitresses. They scare me a bit.

A news piece I saw recently filters into my brain. They are scary as hell, but they also do some good for the community. For example, they help with one of the local shelters and they also help kids face their abusers in court. It's pretty remarkable.

I remember watching the television that day and wishing I had the guts to ask them for help. I convinced myself that I would the next time one of them came into the diner, but that never happened. And now, here I am, with the President right in front of me.

"What's your name?" I ask, my voice a bit shaky.

He stops walking and pivots to face me. "Snow."

"You said only your friends call you Snow." Lennox steps

around Snow and glares at him. "We're not your stupid friends."

"Oh, baby." I rush to my son and drop to my knees. I run my hands over him to check for injuries. He's warm and seems okay. His attitude certainly seems to be in working order. "I was so worried about you."

"I'm fine, Mom."

"I can see that."

"You need to go apologize to Dad so we can go home."

Embarrassment sends heat rushing over my cheeks, and I stand up. I can feel Snow's—or whatever his name is—eyes on me so I look everywhere but at him.

"Son, you might want to rethink that statement."

I whip my head in Snow's direction and narrow my eyes at him. Anger infuses my stare. I agree with his statement, but it's not his place to admonish my child.

"Excuse me, but I—"

"I'm not your damn son."

Lennox and I speak at the same time and while I'm tired, I can't let his last words go.

"Lennox," I snap. "That's not how we talk to people."

"It's how Dad talks," he argues.

"I think your dad needs a lesson in manners," Snow says under his breath.

"While I'm inclined to agree with you," I look pointedly at Snow. "It's up to me to scold my son."

"Lady, it is—"

"Sami," I say, cutting him off. "My name is Sami. Or Samantha. It isn't 'lady.'"

Snow runs his gaze from my face, down the length of my body and back up again before giving a curt nod. "Sami suits you."

His stare warms me in all the places I was still cold. The

way my name rolls off his tongue somehow feels normal, like it was meant to be said only by him. *Weird.*

"His name is Zeke," Lennox says from his position beside me, reminding me that he's there. I didn't forget, not really. "Now can we go home?"

I glance down at him. "No, Lennox, we can't go home." I look back at Snow and then return my attention to Lennox. "Dad had some things to do and needed us to leave for the night."

The lie slips out easily. Lennox may be seven and able to tell that things didn't happen exactly like that, but that doesn't mean I need to hash out everything that did happen in front of him.

A woman steps up to Snow's side. She's young and the way she leans into Snow makes me wonder if there's something there. Her eyes widen when she sees that I'm wrapped in only a blanket, and she clears her throat.

"I've got some clothes that you can wear. I'll go get those and then get you two settled for the night. I'm sure you're exhausted."

Without waiting for a response, she walks away. Snow's gaze tracks her movement until she's out of sight.

"Girlfriend?" I ask, although I have no idea why it matters.

"Heather?" Snow's tone is incredulous. I recognize the name from earlier. "Not even close."

"Does she know that?"

"Heather knows the score."

"The score?"

Snow shifts his gaze to Lennox and then back to me. "Yeah, the score." When he sees that my look of confusion is not diminishing, he narrows his eyes. "I'm not going to get into this shit with the kid here."

I don't argue with him because he's right. Talking about

'the score' in front of Lennox is the last thing I need. I wrap my arm around my son's shoulders.

"If you can just show us where we can sleep, I'd appreciate it." Heather arrives with clothes, and I take them from her. "I'll get changed and after a few hours of rest, we'll be out of here."

Snow nods and starts to walk away. "Follow me." He pauses beside a door in a long hallway. "There's a bathroom where you can change." He nods ahead of him. "And Lennox will be down at the end of the hallway. There are two cots right at the edge of the room that I can set you up with, so you'll be together."

"Thanks," I mumble. "I'll be there in a minute, baby," I say to my son. "Go ahead."

I watch as Snow guides my son away from me. My heart races as I once again review the events of the night. I have no idea what Lennox and I will do in the morning, but one thing is for sure.

We won't be staying here, so close to a man that simultaneously scares the shit out of me and makes me wonder about things I have no business wondering about.

SNOW

"It's colder than a witch's tit out there."

Duck stomps his boots to dislodge the snow and then ruffles his hair to do the same. I called him to pick me up when it was clear that riding my Harley back to the clubhouse wasn't safe. Duck is not only my VP, but he's my best friend. I don't know what I'd do without him.

Try to drive home in the fucking snow.

"Where's Mikey?" I ask after it registers that Duck came alone.

"He was cleaning up the clubhouse after last night," Duck answers about the latest prospect. He shakes his head and chuckles. "Dumb fuck about puked when he started scrubbing at the cum stains on the couch. But he should be here soon."

"Good."

I glance over my shoulder as people start to file out of the shelter. Most only come for a place to sleep, so it's pretty quiet during the day. Perfect time for a prospect to have a shift. My gaze lands on Sami, and I watch as she gently shakes her son's shoulder to wake him. It takes several moments but Lennox finally sits up and rubs his eyes with his little fists.

"Who's that?"

Duck's question breaks the spell she seems to have cast on me. I shift my focus back to him and glare.

"No one," I snap.

"You're gonna have to do better if you want me to believe that."

"Nothing to fucking believe, D." I cross my arms over my chest.

"Great. Then you won't mind if I see if she's hungry. Maybe she'd like some duck for breakfast." I reach out and grip Duck's arm as he tries to stroll past me. He drops his eyes to my hand. "That's what I thought."

"You don't know what you're talking about."

"I know more than you think," he mumbles.

"What's that supposed to mean?"

"It means, brother, that you never stare at any of the women that walk through that door. Shit, you haven't looked at a woman, other than to determine if she's worth the ten minutes it takes to fuck her, since Marlene."

The tension in my muscles intensifies at the mention of my ex. The one time I forgot my own rules, I got fucked. Literally and figuratively. There's a reason that I choose my brothers over women. They understand the meaning of loyalty.

"Is everything set for the drop later?"

"Yeah," Duck says, easily accepting my change in subject. "We'll be six deep, like always."

"Hey, Duck." I turn to see Heather standing next to me, her hands in her pockets and a smile on her face. Duck nods in greeting but doesn't say a word. "Right. Always the strong, silent type."

I can't help the laugh that escapes. Duck is anything but

silent. But when it comes to Heather, he can't string two words together. Not even a simple 'hey Heather'.

"Anyway," Heather says on a sigh and shifts her attention to me. "I'm headed out. Connie just clocked in. See ya next time."

Heather walks out the door, and if I'm not mistaken, I can hear Duck deflate like a balloon.

"What the fuck was that?"

"Nothing," Duck responds.

"Bullshit. You can sweet talk every chick that walks into the clubhouse, but you can't even say 'hi' to Heather."

"Because I don't want in Heather's pants," Duck protests. "What's the point in talking to a woman if it's not gonna end in bed?"

"You're hopeless."

"And you're a—"

"We're not going home, Lennox. Quit asking."

"But where the hell are we gonna go?"

Sami and Lennox's voices dim as they walk past Duck and me and head out the front door. The expression on Duck's face matches the frustration I'm feeling.

"What was that all about?" Duck asks when the two are out of earshot.

"The kid's got a giant chip on his shoulder. Needs to learn how to talk to females, especially the one who gave birth to him."

I turn on my heel and walk away from Duck, not wanting to discuss the pretty mom and her clear issues with her disrespectful son. After she'd put some clothes on last night and laid down on the cot next to her kid, I couldn't help but watch as she tossed and turned and tried to sleep. She didn't get much rest. Only about three hours, if I remember correctly.

"I thought Mikey was on today."

I look up and see Connie sitting at the desk that shelter staff share.

"He should be here any—"

"Yo, Snow!" I whirl around at the sound of Duck hollering my name. "We got trouble."

I rush to the door and barrel through it, following Duck, and as the cold air hits my face, I see Mikey straddling a familiar man in the snow. He pulls his arm back and lands a right hook to the man's jaw, and I know if it weren't for the cushion the snow provides, the man would have cracked his damn skull on the cement.

When I reach Mikey's side, I reach out and yank him off his victim. I shove him back a few steps and he's just stupid enough to keep trying to get past me.

"What the fuck are you doing?" I snarl.

"He was yelling at her and the boy," Mikey says, barely winded from his assault, as he tilts his head toward the building.

I look over my shoulder and see Sami and Lennox standing next to the brick wall. Sami's face is ashen, and her stare is fixed on the man on the ground. I let go of Mikey and kneel down next to the prone figure in the snow.

"Corey, you wanna explain why you're harassing this woman and her son?" I narrow my eyes at him and crack my knuckles. "And keep in mind that if I don't like your answer, the drop later will be cancelled, and you'll no longer have the Satan's Legacy feeding your habit."

"Leave my dad alone!" Lennox yells as he grabs my cut and tries to pull me away. "Get away from him."

A tornado couldn't have knocked me on my ass any faster than his words did. Corey is Lennox's dad? Does that mean he's Sami's husband? Boyfriend? Or is he just a piece of shit baby daddy?

As if she just tuned in to the situation, Sami steps forward and rests her hands on Lennox's shoulders to urge him backward, away from me. I can't tell if the fear in her eyes is for the man lying on the ground or for me.

I make a snap decision and hope it doesn't come back to bite me in the ass.

"Corey, get the fuck outta here," I say and rise to my full height. "We'll talk later."

Corey scrambles to his feet and shoots Sami one last look before turning away and strolling down the street like he didn't get the shit beat out of him. I take a deep breath in an effort to regain my composure before facing Sami.

"How the hell do you know Corey?" she demands the second we make eye contact.

I rub the side of my nose as I try to come up with an answer. I know absolutely nothing about this woman other than she has a son and apparently, she's with a total asshole. I'm guessing she also has no idea just how much danger her choice of men puts her in.

"He's a runner." I settle on telling her the truth. I'd much rather she not know more than she needs to about the business of my club, but I also abhor liars.

"Corey's never run a day in his life," she scoffs.

"No, that's not what I mean." I glance at Lennox for a second before looking back at her. "Why don't we go back inside, and I'll fill you in?"

The wariness in Sami's eyes reminds me of a deer caught in headlights. What she, and the deer, fails to realize is that seeing that look puts the fear of God into me. I never get on my bike with the intention of laying it down on the asphalt because of a damn animal. Same applies to Sami. I don't want to put my club on the line because of what I share with her.

We all traipse inside, and I walk straight to the office on the other side of the building. I know Sami will follow because she wants answers. When we're all seated at the table in the office, I look at Mikey.

"Go out there and start your shift." I glance at Lennox. "Hey, kid. I bet Miss Connie can find you something to eat if you wanna go with Mikey."

Lennox looks at his mom, who nods slightly to grant him permission.

Mikey let's Lennox exit before him, and he slams the door behind him.

Sami jumps at the sound, and I make a mental note to give Mikey hell later. Like Lennox, he needs to learn how to act around women.

"Can you please just tell me how you know Corey?" Sami asks with hesitation in her voice. "I'd like to get Lennox home."

I arch a brow at her. "Where exactly is home?"

"None of your business," she snaps.

"That's where you're wrong." I lean my elbows on the table and lock eyes with Sami. "How well do you know Corey?"

SAMI

How well do you know Corey?

That question echoes in my head as Snow continues to tell me just how much I *don't* know about the man I've been living with for the last eight years. My stomach is in knots, and if I'd eaten anything in the last twelve hours, I know it'd be making an appearance again. I stare at my shaking hands and listen to the deep voice that's ensuring my world crumbles completely.

"Judging by the look on your face, I'm guessing you had no idea what was going on right under your nose."

I whip my head up and lock eyes with Snow, expecting to see judgement in the green depths. Instead, all I see is anger.

"We don't know each other, so I'm going to forgive you for insinuating that I'd raise my son in the environment you're describing." I wring my hands in front of me. "No, I didn't know." I force the words past the lump in my throat.

"Look, I'm not trying to make you uncomfortable." Snow reaches across the table and rests his hands on mine, calming the shaking. "And I know I'm practically a stranger, but—"

"A stranger who's seen me naked," I mumble under my breath.

"Wait… what?"

I lift my head and look at the other man in the room. I'd forgotten he was there, he'd been so quiet. His jaw would be on the floor if it were possible, and warmth floods my cheeks as embarrassment sets in.

"Shut your damn mouth, Duck," Snow demands of his friend.

Duck's mouth slowly closes but not for long. "When did you see her naked?" He's talking as if I'm not even in the room, and my embarrassment morphs into anger.

"I'm right here," I snap. I glare at both men before answering Duck's question. "He felt the need to strip me down and toss me into a bath last night."

"You're leaving out some pretty important details, don't ya think?" Snow asks with one brow arched. "Like how you were passed out in the snow, in the middle of the night, and you were freezing. And how I only took your clothes off because they were cold and wet, and I needed to get your body temp up. Oh, and let's not forget about how my actions worked."

I wave my hand dismissively. "Yeah, fine."

Duck chuckles and shakes his head. "Well, I'd say my brother here," he tilts his head at Snow, "did what he had to in order to make sure you were okay."

I heave a sigh. Clearly, they aren't going to see things the way I do, and I get the feeling that no amount of arguing will make a difference.

"Can we please get back to the issue at hand?"

"Sure," Snow concedes. "Let's talk about where you and Lennox are going to go when you leave here."

"That's none of your concern."

"That's where you're wrong, angel. I just got done telling

25

you that your boyfriend has been running drugs for Satan's Legacy and you say you're gonna go home. I don't think so."

"You're Satan's Legacy!" I shout, shooting up from my chair.

"Chick's got a point," Duck says.

"Shut up, Duck," Snow barks.

With rage fueling my every movement, I hustle around the table toward the door. Snow snakes his arm out and grips my upper arm, spinning me around to face him.

"Where are you going?"

"I repeat, none of your concern."

"I don't think you're getting what I'm telling you." Snow drops my arm and takes a step back. "Corey is dangerous. More dangerous than any of the Satan's Legacy brothers ever could be, at least where you're concerned."

I narrow my eyes at him and cross my arms over my chest. "Explain."

"Corey kicked you and your son out in the freezing cold. I'm going to guess, based on the way he likes to run his mouth, that this isn't the first time and if you go back, it wouldn't be the last." Snow looks at me as if waiting for confirmation and when I remain silent, he continues. "Satan's Legacy may be full of some fucking rough guys, but we'd never hurt a woman or child."

"And I'm supposed to believe that?"

What he doesn't know is I do believe it. I've lived in Denver my entire life, and while Satan's Legacy strikes fear in the hearts of everyone, me included, I can appreciate what they've done for the community. And throughout all of the news reports, their name has never been linked with anything involving a woman and child in a negative way.

"I don't give a damn what you believe. Corey just got a beating and I have no doubt he's going to take it out on you if you go home."

I think about Snow's words and realize that maybe he's right. Corey has never been physically violent, at least not until he put his hands on my throat last night. Now that he's crossed that line, I know it's not long before he does it again… or worse.

I look between Snow and Duck, contemplating my options. Hard to do when I have no options. Not a single one. I have nowhere else to go but home. I can't traipse around the city with Lennox in tow, and I have no family or friends. Corey made sure of that.

"What do you suggest?" I ask with trepidation.

Snow settles on the table, arms crossed over his chest. He looks toward Duck, who gives a slight nod and refocuses his attention on me.

"Why don't you and Lennox come back to the clubhouse with me?"

"You can't be serious."

"Uh, Pres, shouldn't this be put to a vote?"

Duck and I speak at the same time. My mouth slams shut at his words because maybe, just maybe, he's said the one thing that will knock some sense into Snow.

"Why would I have to put it to a vote?" Snow snarls. "I'm the fucking president."

"Exactly," Duck says calmly. "If another brother brought a woman and child to the clubhouse without a vote, you'd be the first to punish them and you know it."

Snow heaves a sigh and drops his chin. When he raises his head, he looks at me and flashes a smile that would melt the panties of lesser women.

"You'll have to excuse my VP." He glares at Duck for a split second before returning his eyes to mine. "He's forgotten his place."

"Look," I start. "I don't want to cause trouble and I certainly don't think that moving into your clubhouse is the best option." I force a smile of my own. "I'll figure something out."

I walk around the table only to be blocked from leaving the room by Snow. I narrow my eyes at him and try to step around his massive frame.

"You're not walking out that door," Snow barks.

"Snow…" Duck's tone holds a hint of warning, although based on their power dynamic, I'm not sure it will hold any sway.

"What?"

"Maybe give her a say in where she goes?" Duck's words are phrased as a question, but something tells me that Snow won't see it that way.

"Why don't you go get the van warmed up?" Snow counters. "We'll be out in a minute."

Snow doesn't look away from me as he speaks to Duck. I swallow down the fear he's inciting and lick my lips. The door clicks shut behind Duck, causing me to flinch.

"I really need to get going so if you'll just—"

"I've got shit to do so why don't we skip the same song and dance, and we can both get outta here?" Snow arches a brow to punctuate his statement.

"I'm not going to your clubhouse." I wave a hand dismissively. "Or whatever you call it."

"And you can't go back to Corey."

I let out a humorless laugh. "Yeah, you've made that abundantly clear."

Snow's brows furrow and he shakes his head. "What can I do to convince you to come with us?"

That's the last thing I expected to hear him say. Wary of his motives, I search his eyes for any hint of manipulation and find none. There's heat, resignation, frustration… but no manipulation.

I take a deep breath and hold it for what feels like forever but is really only a few seconds. I know my answer isn't going to make a damn bit of sense to him, especially when it doesn't to me, but it's the first thing that popped into my head when he asked the question and in some weird way, it's true.

"Let me go."

SNOW

"*S*it the fuck down and shut up!"

I look to my right and notice Duck is coiled tighter than a rattler ready to strike, which is fitting considering it mirrors my own demeanor. I scan the room and take in the faces of Satan's Legacy MC, my brothers, as they do what they're told. Each man is wearing their cut, which is mandatory for church, and the skull with devil horns patch matches the large painted logo on the wall.

"What the patch binds together, let no force tear apart. Satan's Legacy now and forever."

The club motto echoes around the room as the patched members repeat it. There's pride in the words, in what they stand for. Every single one of us is here because we want to be. Satan's Legacy is our chosen family and provides more than any blood ties ever could.

"Before we rehash the plan for today's drop, there's something you need to know," I begin. "Duck seems to think I should put this to a vote, but that's not going to happen." I look around the room and meet each man's eyes. "You voted me in as President and because of that, I trust that you'll back me on this no matter what."

"What's with the fucking cloak and dagger speech, Pres?" Toga asks from his seat to my left. "You know we got your back."

"Good." I give a sharp nod. "There's going to be a woman and her son staying with us for a while." Shocked expressions and hushed murmurs are the only response I get. Glasses rattle when my fist connects with the wooden table. "Listen up!" I shout to get their attention. "This isn't up for debate, and I expect you to make them feel comfortable and give them the respect they deserve."

"Uh, Pres, I'm pretty sure they didn't agree to stay here," Duck reminds me.

All eyes shift to him and the confusion on my men's faces would be comical in any other situation.

"They'll be here. Trust me," I say, recalling the last words I said to Sami.

"Let me go."

"Fine." I turn away from her and open the door to head toward the van.

Sami follows, like I knew she would. I know she's doing what she feels she needs to. She's being a mama bear. But when she sees that my club is the lesser of two evils, she'll come around.

When we reach the front door of the shelter, I stop and glance over my shoulder. "Wait here."

I step out into the snowy cold and rush to the van to grab what I need. Duck looks at me and opens his mouth to speak, but I slam the door shut before he can get a word out. I stride back inside and hold back the grin when I see Sami standing in the same place.

"Here." I thrust the handful of quarters and a slip of paper at her.

"What is it?" she asks, eyeing the device in my outstretched palm.

31

"It's change and my phone number."

"No shit," she snaps. "I mean, why are you giving it to me?"

"Because you're going to wish you'd taken me up on my offer, and when you do, I want you to be able to get a hold of me."

"You're pushy, you know that?" She crosses her arms over her chest, ignoring the money.

"Keeps me and my club alive and riding."

"Also makes you a jerk."

"I've been called worse." I chuckle but at her sharp look, I force myself to stop. I realize that she's not going to make this easy, so I make a snap decision. I reach forward and pull out her front jeans pocket, depositing the quarters and paper inside. I do it so quickly that she doesn't have a chance to stop me.

"When you come to your senses, call me. Doesn't matter what time it is, I'll come. No questions asked."

With that, I walk away from Sami, knowing she'll do what she needs to do to keep Lennox safe, even if she's not worried about her own ass.

"How are we gonna conduct business with some brat here?"

I whip my head in the direction of Brady. He's one of the few of us not married with kids, and it shows. It also seems he's forgotten that women and children are sacred here. Sure, we've got club whores and not all of the married men let the band on their fingers stop them from partaking, but that doesn't change the fact that they love their families, that they would do whatever it takes to protect them.

"I'm going to fucking pretend I didn't just hear that come outta your mouth," I bark. When I calm my temper, I continue. "We conduct business as usual. Nothing changes that. Besides, they're my problem, not yours. I'm telling you about Sami and Lennox out of respect, not because it's up for debate."

"You know I didn't mean anything bad, Pres," Brady says,

scrambling to cover his ass. "But we've got a lot going on this month, with the shifts at the shelter, the toy drive and holiday stuff we do. And let's not forget this drop today with Corey. A lot is riding on that and if something, or *someone*, screws that up, we're fucked."

"Sami is Corey's girlfriend, and Lennox is his son."

"Shit, Pres," Brady huffs. "You shoulda led with that." He strokes his beard and rocks back in his chair, almost toppling it over.

"Maybe," I concede. I rest my elbows on the table and lean forward. "But it shouldn't matter."

"Look, Snow, we get that," Toga starts, glancing around the room and eliciting nods from each member. "But *who* they are changes everything. Corey's a loose cannon on a good day. I can only imagine what he's like at home, when he doesn't have us there to keep him in line."

"Exactly." I rise from my chair. "That leads me to the next order of business. Today's drop."

Duck stands and starts to pace. "We were planning on riding six deep, but I think, in light of our potential house guests, we need to adjust." Duck locks eyes with me and I nod, encouraging him to continue to lay out what we discussed on the ride home from the shelter. "Snow needs to stay here in case Sami calls. That leaves me, Toga, Brady, Dip, and Magic."

"Corey got his ass beat this morning by Mikey so he's gonna be on edge." I glance at Magic, whose grin widens. "You're gonna have to do what you do."

Magic is our Enforcer and earned his road name because of the way he can sweet talk his way through anything, make a fucker believe he's your best friend while simultaneously making them wish they were dead. Simply put, he's pure magic, and vital as hell to our success.

"You got it," Magic agrees, way too happy about his job.

"Don't let your guard down with him. He may seem preoccupied with what went down this morning, but mark my words, he's smarter than he looks. Hell, he's smarter than even he gives himself credit for."

Satan's Legacy has been trying for years to find a way to get on law enforcement's good side, or at least get them to look the other way so we can conduct business, and Corey's the key to that. He has no clue we know, but he's been an informant for years. We've spent all this time feeding him info that keeps us in the clear. Now we just need to switch things up. And if that doesn't work, we'll take him out ourselves. What the patch binds together, let no force tear apart. Satan's Legacy now and forever. And the cops will have to find a new snitch.

"I don't trust him," Toga says, taking the words right out of my mouth.

"Neither do I, but we need him."

"Do we?" Dip questions.

"I'm open to suggestions." I lean forward with my palms flat on the table. "If anyone has any ideas on how we can reach our ultimate goal without Corey, now is the time to speak up."

The room erupts in conversation as we spend the next hour going over any and all options. By the time church is over, a new plan is hatched, and while dangerous, if it works it'll set up Satan's Legacy to expand in ways we never thought possible. Satisfied that we're not only taking care of us but a mother and son too, I smile broadly.

"Meeting adjourned."

SAMI

"I wanna go home."

I grip Lennox's hand tighter, frustration flowing through my fingers. We left the shelter a few hours ago, shortly after Snow. The quarters he dumped in my pocket are burning into my thigh, silently begging to be used.

"That's not gonna happen, baby," I respond for what feels like the millionth time in the last twenty minutes.

"I'm not a baby!" he shouts. Lennox digs his heels into the snow, forcing me to stop walking.

"Lennox," I say through clenched teeth. "We need to keep walking."

As the words leave my mouth, I realize I have no idea where we're going. I want to go home just as much as he does, although for very different reasons. Lennox wants to see his dad, and I get it, but I don't give a shit if I never see Corey again. But I do need to get some things from the house.

Maybe if you call Snow, he could go with you.

I shove that thought out of my head, angry that my brain

is betraying me. I don't need Snow. I don't need anyone other than Lennox. He may hate me now, but someday, he'll thank me for making the hard decisions.

"I'm hungry," Lennox whines, pulling me from my musings.

My stomach growls, reminding me that we haven't eaten since breakfast at the shelter. I don't have any money, other than the quarters Snow gave me, and that's not enough for both of us to eat. But it just may be enough to get Lennox a sandwich.

"C'mon," I say, injecting as much cheer into my tone as possible. "Let's find you something to eat."

Lennox and I walk another two blocks before we reach a McDonald's. I breathe a sigh of relief when I see that it's one with the playground inside. Lennox can eat and we can both get warm. And hopefully, I can sort out a plan for what to do next while he plays.

Warm air hits my face when we step inside, and my cheeks tingle at the sudden change in temperature. I point to the play area and urge Lennox in that direction so I can order without him there. He doesn't need to see his mama paying in change and I don't need him begging me for more than I can afford.

"Welcome to McDonald's." The cashier greets me with a smile. "What can I get you today?"

"I'd like, um…" I pull the change out of my pocket and dump it on the counter, too tired to hold on to my pride any longer. "Is this enough for a happy meal?"

The woman eyes me for a moment before scraping the coins into her hand and counting what's there. I silently count along with her.

"There's more than enough," she lies. "In fact, you've got some left over."

She hands me back four quarters. Tears burn the back of

my eyes, and I can't stop them from spilling over my lashes. "Thank you," I choke out.

"Don't mention it, honey." She winks at me as she rings up the order.

I step away from the counter and wait for Lennox's food. I can hear his laughter from the play area, and I look over my shoulder at him. He's playing with another little boy and he's happy.

When my order number is called, I pick up the tray and notice there's more food than I ordered, along with a steaming cup of coffee. I look at the cashier, and when she smiles, I mouth the words 'thank you'. It's been a long time since I've been on the receiving end of such kindness.

Snow was kind to you just a few hours ago.

I make my way to a table and call Lennox over to eat. He mutters under his breath about how he'd rather play, but when he opens his happy meal, he forgets all about the mini jungle gym and his new friend.

I watch as he eats his fries and chicken nuggets like he's starving. The sight is a sucker punch to the gut, and I have to look away so he doesn't see my tears.

My gaze lands on something silver on the street corner and I stare. If ever I needed a sign to tell me what to do, seeing something practically extinct just might be it. The voice in my head screams at me to suck up my pride one more time and go use the payphone to call Snow. She demands that I remember that I'd be making that phone call for Lennox, not myself.

I want to argue with her, tell her to screw herself, but I know it wouldn't do any good. That woman is the only voice of reason I have left. And she's right. This is about my son, not me. Besides, I can't keep him fed and warm with only a dollar to my name.

"Lennox," I say, returning my attention to him. "Mommy's

gonna go make a call." I point to the phone booth on the corner. "Do not move until I get back, okay?"

Lennox nods, his mouth too full to speak. I stand up from the chair and take a deep breath before forcing my feet to carry me outside and to the phone. I insert two quarters and dial the number on the slip of paper Snow gave me.

The phone rings and just when I think no one is going to answer, the ringing stops.

"'Lo.'"

Snow's deep, gravelly voice curls around me, settling my nerves. Crazy how one syllable from a man I barely know can have that effect.

"Um, Snow?" Nerves, along with the cold, whip through me. "This is—"

"Sami," he says.

"Uh, yeah." I roll my eyes at myself because apparently, I'm incapable of coherent speech at the moment.

"Good job, Angel."

"What?"

"You're doing the right thing." He chuckles. "I'm proud of you. Means you're a good mama and care more about that boy of yours than you do your pride."

Taken aback by his praise, I remain silent. No one has ever told me they're proud of me and I've certainly never heard that I'm a good mom.

"Where are you?"

"I, um…" I look around me to find the street sign. "The phone booth outside of McDonald's on Federal."

"Got it. Go back inside and stay warm. I'll be there in twenty."

The line goes dead, and I hold the phone away from my ear and stare at it. Seriously? That was much easier than I was expecting. I thought I'd have to listen to an entire speech about how he told me so, but no. He did exactly what he promised.

He's coming, no questions asked.

SNOW

I pull my truck into the McDonald's parking lot and am surprised to see Sami and Lennox standing outside in the cold. I can see Sami's jaw twitch as her teeth chatter, and her slender body shakes with her shivers. Lennox is bundled up in the same jacket he had on when they arrived at the shelter, but he's wearing a hat that I recognize as Mikey's.

"What the hell are you doing out in the freezing cold?" I ask after I park and roll my window down. "C'mon. Hop in."

Sami eyes me warily but quickly shuffles Lennox to the passenger side and helps him up into the cab of the truck. He scoots toward the middle but stops short of actually bumping into me. Sami climbs in and slams the door shut behind her.

I wait for them to put on their seatbelts and then pull out of the parking lot, pointing the truck in the direction of their house. They're going to need more clothes if they're gonna be staying at the clubhouse. Corey won't be home because of his meeting with my guys, so it's perfect timing.

"I thought you said we were going to the clubhouse."

Sami's tone holds a hint of fear and I hate that. I glance at her and notice her eyes are wide and she's leaning forward, straining against the seatbelt as if she's preparing to run. Lennox, on the other hand, looks excited. Dammit!

"I figured you'd want some of your own stuff," I say, my tone calm and even. When Sami's hand shifts from her lap to the door, I add, "He's not home."

Her head whips in my direction. "How do you know?"

"Trust me, okay angel?"

She opens her mouth to speak and presses her lips together, stopping whatever words there were. I park next to the curb in front of the rundown house and look at the structure with a fresh perspective. Of course, I've seen the house before. I never thought about how dilapidated it was until right this minute. Corey has mentioned a girl and kid several times, but he's a junkie and I didn't believe him.

You should have.

Regret sits heavily on my shoulders as I get out of the truck and walk around to help Sami down. She ignores my outstretched hand and jumps down herself, turning to lift Lennox out. I can tell that his weight is almost too much for her, but I say nothing. She doesn't trust me and she's stubborn. I'll win her over somehow, but it won't be by taking away her ability to be a parent to her son.

"Let's try to make this quick, okay?"

Sami nods and scurries past me, making her way to the front door. Her feet are buried by snow with each step she takes, and I struggle not to pick her up and carry her. Instead, I focus on the way her jeans hug her ass and her hips sway with her quick movements. Reminding myself that there's a kid present, I slyly adjust myself and turn to see Lennox standing next to me, staring up at me with judgement in his eyes.

"What?"

"You can go now."

I arch a brow. He has grit, I'll give him that. He's loyal to his dad and disrespectful as hell toward his mom. I can appreciate the loyalty, but the disrespect has to go.

"I could but I'm not." I put my hand on his shoulder and urge him toward the house. He resists, but I'm stronger and I don't let up. "Let's get your stuff."

Lennox breaks away from me and runs up the walkway and through the front door, slamming it behind him. I hear a lock engage and shake my head in disbelief. The little shit locked me out. I could easily kick the door in, and while I'm tempted, I know it won't win me any points.

I hear Sami's voice through the rickety wooden barrier, and just as I raise my fist to knock, the door flies open. Sami has an armful of what I assume are clothes and she's scolding Lennox for shutting me out.

"I'm sorry," she says and steps back so I can enter. "Lennox has been—"

I hold a hand up to stop her. "Don't apologize for him." She narrows her eyes at me, and I drop my hand. "Dammit, Angel, you take everything wrong. I'm not telling you what to do."

"Coulda fooled me," she mumbles.

"Look, I'm not saying that an apology isn't warranted, but it should be from him." When she opens her mouth to argue, I place my flattened palm over her lips. Her eyes widen and my shoulders tense as electricity ricochets through me at the contact. "And yes, I know he's only seven, but he needs to learn somehow. That being said, I respect his loyalty to his dad, even if the man is a scumbag." I remove my hand from her mouth and shift it to cup her cheek. "And you deserve to be treated better by your son."

Sami's eyes soften, and if I'm not mistaken, she leans into my touch. How long has it been since this woman has felt cherished? Probably too long. I may be rough around the edges, but if she'd let me, I'd show her just how soft I can be. Without thinking, I lean forward, maintaining eye contact and—

"Stop touching my mom!"

Sami and I are startled away from each other by Lennox's shout. I suck in a ragged breath, frustrated that I let myself get carried away. Sami's face is flushed, and I can't help but wonder if embarrassment is the cause or if she wanted what almost happened as much as I did.

"Lennox," Sami admonishes in what I would call a true mom voice.

"It's okay Angel," I say to Sami while my full attention is on Lennox. "I've got this. Why don't you go finish gathering whatever you want to take?"

Sami looks from her son to me and back again. "Be nice," she demands. She spares me one last glance before she takes off down the hall toward what I can only assume is a bedroom.

"Have a seat," I instruct Lennox.

Lennox doesn't move. He glares at me in only a way a child can, and for a second, I feel guilty. It's a fleeting second because I remind myself that he's a kid and I'm the adult, and whether I'm his dad or not, he needs to be respectful.

I take a step toward him, and when he jolts backward as if he's scared, I stop. Lennox looks around the room, at anything and everything but me. I hate that he's been in a position to feel this way, and while I don't understand it, I can appreciate that it's going to take more than me wanting to teach him some manners to be what he needs.

Protectiveness, unlike anything I've ever felt before, grabs ahold of my soul and doesn't let go. It hits me that I want Lennox to not only feel safe with me, but I want him to *like* me. Shit, I want his mother to like me. I've volunteered so much of my adult life at shelters and with charities that focus on families and children, but I've never wanted to be more than a friendly face to any of them. For whatever reason, Sami and Lennox are different. They have been since the moment I opened that door and laid eyes on them for the first time.

"Lennox, will you please sit?" I ask, having decided to change tactics.

He narrows his eyes at me and shuffles his feet for a few minutes before he drags himself to the couch and plops down. My gaze focuses in on his feet, hanging a few inches off the floor. We sit in silence for a moment while I gather my thoughts. Nothing about finding common ground with him is going to be easy, and honestly, it shouldn't be. He's right… I'm a stranger. But not for long.

"Why are you still here?" he asks, breaking the silence.

"Well," I begin and rub the back of my neck. "I want to make sure you and your mom are safe, and to do that, I need to stay with you."

Lennox glances at me out of the corner of his eyes and huffs out a breath. "We don't need you."

Everything in me wants to argue, wants to correct him and remind him that his father kicked them out into the cold, but I refrain. It won't get me anywhere.

"Probably not," I concede. "But I like to help people."

"Why?" he scoffs. "Helping people is stupid."

"Ya think?" I counter and he nods. "Now, who told you it's stupid?"

"My dad."

Of course he did. If there's one thing about Corey I'm certain of, it's that he's never helped anyone other than himself in his miserable life.

"And you agree with your dad?"

"Duh."

"Let me ask you this, then." I shift on the couch so I'm facing him. "Was it stupid when you were banging on the door last night to get help for your mom?"

Lennox seems to think about it for a moment and sighs dramatically. "No, I guess not."

His tone is sullen, and I have to stifle the laugh threatening to escape. "And is there any other times when you've helped someone and it wasn't stupid?"

"No," he answers quickly.

"Hmmm…" I run my fingers over my beard. "What about a few minutes ago when you yelled at me to stop touching her? Weren't you doing that to help your mom?"

"Maybe," he mumbles.

"It seems to me that helping people isn't always stupid. Right?"

"I guess."

Lennox finally shifts to face me, bringing his knees up so he's resting on them. He looks at me for a long moment before opening his mouth to speak.

"Now what?" he asks.

"Now, I think you should give your mom a hand and make sure she's getting everything you guys need to bring with you."

"What are you gonna do?"

"I'm going to stand at the front door and wait."

"What if my dad comes home? He's not gonna be happy if he sees you here."

No shit.

"Don't worry about that," I say and ruffle his hair. He doesn't flinch away from me. "Just go help your mom, and maybe, if she says it's okay, we can do something fun after we leave."

His eyes light up. "Like what?"

"Don't know yet." I stand from the couch. "Why don't you

think about what you'd want to do and we'll talk it over when we leave."

"You promise?"

"As long as it's something your mom is okay with, yeah." I nod. "I promise."

Lennox scrambles from the couch and thrusts a fist in the air and whisper shouts, "Yes!"

I watch him disappear down the same hall as Sami and wonder what I've just gotten myself into. Not that it matters. I made a promise.

Come hell or high water, I fucking keep my promises.

SAMI

"*A*re we there yet?"

Lennox wiggles toward the edge of his seat. He's between Snow and me with only a lap belt for safety, and I wrap my arm around his shoulders to try to hold him still. My fingertips brush Snow's arm, and I quickly clench my fist to break the contact.

"Almost," Snow chuckles.

He's been very patient with Lennox since they chatted back at the house. I don't know exactly what was said, but my son has been more polite in the last hour than he has since he started idolizing his dad, so I'll take it as a win.

Snow navigates the roads with ease. The roads outside of the city are treacherous with Denver's harsh winter conditions. Normally, I'd be shaking like a leaf, but with Snow, I'm not. There's something about him that makes me believe that Lennox and I are safe… and not just on the roads.

He turns left onto an unmarked road and drives for another half mile before stopping at a closed gate. Snow lifts his cell phone from the dash and taps the screen a few times.

The gate swings open and he pulls through. I quickly glance over my shoulder to see the gate close behind us.

Snow shifts the truck into four-wheel drive as he approaches a hill and when we reach the top, the land seems to open up before us. Below us is what appears to be a valley, something I'm not used to seeing living in the city. Buildings dot the expanse of land in a circle, with a larger building in the middle.

Lennox's eyes widen at the sight, as do mine.

"This looks more like a military compound than a club-house," I remark, weariness in my tone.

"Exactly," Snow agrees, pulling my gaze from the view to his face. "We have many enemies, Angel. We do what's necessary to protect our own."

"I see."

But I don't see. I don't understand. Why, if they're good people, do they stay so hidden? Why do they have enemies? *Who* are their enemies?

"You don't, but you will."

Snow winks at me and butterflies dance in my stomach. I pull Lennox into my side, as if that alone will protect him from whatever we're driving into. It's ludicrous, really. Snow has been nothing but kind to me and my son.

And even though the club has always caused fear to skate up my spine when they walk through the door at the diner, they've never done anything to deserve that reaction. They're friendly enough, polite. Rowdy, too, but that doesn't equal scary.

"Where are we gonna stay?" Lennox asks as Snow drives the truck down the hill.

"There." Snow points to our right. "That's my place. But we're gonna stop at the clubhouse first."

"I thought you said we were staying at the clubhouse?" I ask, suddenly questioning my sanity for agreeing to this.

Snow shrugs. "We refer to the whole place as the club-house. We don't like outsiders knowing we have our own houses on site."

"But why?"

"Because they don't need to know," he replies simply, as if I should have figured that out on my own. When I stare at him, he explains. "If an enemy gets past our security and manages to get this far, we'd rather they think they're only up against a few members, not the whole club."

"But…" I shake my head. "Doesn't that put the families in danger? If someone gets this far, the whole club is at risk, right?"

"Looks can be deceiving."

"What the hell is that supposed to mean?" I demand.

"You'll see," Snow says cryptically.

Lennox tugs out of my grasp and glares at me. "Quit being mean to him!" he shouts.

The truck lurches to a stop, and Snow flips it into park before twisting in his seat to look at Lennox. My son shrinks into me a little, but his body remains stiff.

"I thought we talked about this," Snow says, his tone calm, even. "Your mother might let you get away with that attitude, but here, on my property, you'll follow my rules."

"You're not my dad!" Lennox yells. "I want my dad!"

Snow rests a hand on Lennox's shoulder. I watch in fasci-nation as he and Lennox stare one another down, Lennox finally heaving a sigh.

"Fine, I'll follow the rules," he grumbles.

"And?" Snow prods as he arches a brow.

Lennox tips his head to look at me. "Sorry."

Snow ruffles my son's hair and turns back to drive again. "Just so we're clear, as long as you're here, you'll be respectful to all adults. Got it?"

"Got it," Lennox mumbles.

49

"Good."

Lennox sits up straight. "Do I still get to pick something fun to do? Since I said 'sorry'?"

Snow grins. "As long as your mama says it's okay, yes." He quickly glances at Lennox. "Since you apologized."

Snow pulls in front of the building centered in the circle. It's a concrete structure, painted black with a red emblem that's identical to the one on Snow's cut. He helps us out of the truck and leads us to a steel door, where he punches a code into the keypad to the right of it. The door swings open, much like the gate did, and we step inside.

My breath hitches at the difference between the outside and inside. We're greeted by several club members and introduced to two women who are called ol' ladies. A little boy, about the same age as Lennox, runs up to us and stops short of colliding with Snow's legs.

"Whoa," Snow says as he bends to the boy's eye level. "Where's the fire, Shiloh?"

Shiloh's face scrunches up like he's thinking about the question, and then he smiles. "There's no fire." He playfully smacks Snow's arm. "Mommy told me you were bringing me a new friend to play with."

"Ah, okay." Snow straightens. "Give Uncle Zeke some time to show them around, and then you can play." He glances at my son. "If Lennox wants to play, and if his mom says it's okay."

Uncle Zeke?

Shiloh's shoulders slump. "'Kay. I'll wait."

Snow laughs. "Thanks buddy. Why don't you go watch some TV until we're done?"

Shiloh takes off running, and I feel Lennox try to pull away from me to follow. "You can play in a bit, okay?" I say to him.

He nods, but a quick glance at his face tells me he doesn't

want to wait. Too bad. I need time to take in our temporary home before I let him out of my sight.

When I look back at Snow, he's standing with his feet braced apart and his arms crossed over his chest. He's watching me, and I can't help but wonder what he's thinking. The silence threatens to swallow me whole, so I break it.

"So, you're an uncle?" I ask awkwardly.

He arches a brow for a moment before his face relaxes into a grin. "Good for you, Angel."

Confusion rushes to the forefront of my thoughts. "Huh?"

"Most people can't accept the race difference. You didn't even comment on it."

"I, ah…" *Seriously?* "I guess I just don't see why it matters."

"Like I said, good for you." Snow drops his arms to his sides and sighs. "Shiloh's had a rough time of it. Kids can be cruel with their questions and their teasing. Shit, most adults are just as bad."

"Trust me, I know how awful people can be," I comment, thinking back on my own childhood. I was the poor girl from the wrong side of the tracks. I don't know who was worse… kids my own age or my parents. It doesn't matter. I can't change it.

"I'm sorry you know what that's like," Snow says, a genuineness in his tone. "Anyway, Shiloh was abandoned at birth. Went into the foster care system for a while before landing in placement with my sister. Now, he's one of us and always will be."

Anger and awe war in my heart. I can't imagine abandoning Lennox, no matter how difficult being a parent is at times. And trust me, it's damn difficult. But he's my son, and I wouldn't change that for anything.

The fact that Snow's sister took Shiloh in, so selflessly, and he's welcomed with open arms by everyone, makes my heart happy. There's a lot of evil in this world, and after the last however many hours since Corey kicked us out, it's refreshing to see that it hasn't inflicted everybody.

I swallow past the lump in my throat and nod. "He seems like a sweet kid."

"He really is," Snow says and squares his shoulders. "But enough about my family. Why don't we get you settled so Lennox can play if he wants?"

"Yes!" Lennox shouts, pumping his fist in the air.

His exuberance cuts through the weird tension and both Snow and I laugh. "Sounds like a plan."

Snow leads us back outside, where we grab our belongings from the truck. We walk the short distance to his place, and its cream siding and black shutters are a little more welcoming than the concrete clubhouse. The home isn't huge, but it's definitely bigger than where Lennox and I lived with Corey.

Snow unlocks the front door and pushes it open before stepping aside so we can go in first. When he closes the door and locks us in, he turns to face us.

"Welcome home," he says, a little awkwardly. When I say nothing, his face falls. "Or, to *my* home."

I spin in a circle to take in the furnishings. It's surprisingly... homey. There's a leather sectional facing a large flat screen TV, which hangs above a fireplace. I can see into the kitchen, which is separated from the living space by a peninsula. The rooms are painted in dark colors, but it still feels inviting somehow. Snow really seemed to do a lot with a little.

"Where am I gonna sleep?" Lennox asks.

"There are two rooms with a shared bathroom down that hall." He points to the left. "And my room is on the other side of the house."

Lennox takes off toward the two rooms, throwing doors open when he reaches them.

"I want this one," he calls out to us.

Snow chuckles. "That would be the one that Shiloh uses when he stays with me. It's got all the toys."

"Ah." I shuffle my feet before locking eyes with him. "I don't want to put Shiloh out of a room. Lennox and I can share."

Snow takes a step in my direction, then another. Oxygen seems to disappear the closer he gets. "Angel, it's fine. I want you both to make yourselves at home while you're here."

"You know this is temporary, right?" I remind him. "Just until we sort this out with Corey. I'll find us a place to live."

"Sure… yeah." He nods. "I know. But in the meantime, consider this your home." He rushes to add, "Until things get sorted out."

"Thank you."

"You're very—"

A knock sounds on the door, cutting him off.

"Zeke," a very pissed off female voice calls through the barrier, causing Snow to roll his eyes. "Open the door. It's cold as shit out here."

Snow begins to walk backward, toward the door, but speaks to me. "Go settle in with Lennox. Make yourselves at home while I deal with this."

I can't stop the twinge of jealousy that Snow is dismissing me to 'deal with' another woman, and I hate myself for it.

I turn on my heel and rush down the same hall Lennox did, entering the first room I come to and slamming the door behind me. I flip the lock, spin around to lean against the wood, and slide down to the floor.

Get a grip, Sami. He's not yours to get jealous over.

SNOW

I yank open the door and glare at Laney, who's standing with her fist raised, poised to knock again... if you can call her pounding a knock.

My sister pushes past me, into the living room, and I swallow the groan that crawls up my throat. I don't know what has her in a tizzy, but I'm guessing it has to do with my houseguests. She may have kept her ire from her son, in an effort to keep him from worrying, but all that means is she's saved it all for me.

"You can't keep a woman and child here, Zeke," Laney says hotly, looking around as if Sami and Lennox are going to jump out from the shadows.

"Keep your voice down," I snap, sparing a quick glance at the guest bedrooms before returning my attention to her. "You'll scare them."

"I don't care!" she shouts, and when I narrow my eyes at her, she continues a little more quietly. "What the hell were you thinking?"

I stalk toward Laney and grab her by the arm to drag her toward my room on the opposite side of the house. She struggles against my hold, but she and I both know it's in vain. I shove her through the doorway and slam the door closed behind us.

Laney crosses her arms over her chest and glares daggers at me.

"What the fuck is your problem?" I bark.

"My problem?" she huffs. "Jesus, I know you're not this stupid. What do you even know about this chick?"

"I know she's a single mother, down on her luck. I know her baby daddy is a piece of shit runner for the club, and he treats her like trash." I close my eyes and tip my head back. "I know them staying here is not up for discussion and not even close to any of your business."

"That's where you're wrong," she snaps. "This is my home too, my family you're putting in danger by having them here."

"How the hell are they putting you in danger?"

"That," she says as she stabs a finger at my chest. "That attitude right there is how. You've always been a sucker for a sob story. And I'll give you this, sometimes that's a good thing, but in this case…" Laney heaves a sigh as she steps back and lets her arms fall to her sides.

"What?" I ask. "What about 'in this case'?"

I'm pretty sure I know what has her going off the rails, but maybe I'm wrong. I hope I'm wrong because I don't know how to fix it if I'm not.

"Don't," she mumbles. "Just please don't do this."

I step toward her, and when she doesn't retreat, I wrap my arm around her and haul her into my chest. Laney's body relaxes and she leans into me as she begins to tremble. I expel all of my frustration on a sigh and smooth a hand over her hair.

"This isn't like that, ya know?"

She shakes her head and sniffles.

"Cedric is never coming back," I remind her. "He's dead, Laney. He can't hurt you or Shi ever again."

My sister pushes away from me and swipes at the tears under her eyes. "I know that," she admits. "But I didn't want him here in the first place."

I shove my hands in my pockets. "Don't you think I know that?" I argue. "Does it ever occur to you that I think about the fact that I convinced you to give him a chance, that I invited him to live here because I thought it would be good for Shiloh to have his biological dad around?" I start to pace. "I beat myself up every fucking day for that!"

"Then why is it so easy for you to do it again, to invite perfect strangers to live here?"

"Because it's the right thing to do." I stop to stand in front of her again. "And I'll remind you, I may have been the first to fuck up where Cedric was concerned, but I wasn't the one who fell in love with him. I wasn't the one who was going to bind myself to him forever because I had goddamn stars in my eyes!"

When Laney's fist fits perfectly into my eye socket, I regret my outburst. It's not the first time she's let her anger get the better of her and punched me, but it is the first time I truly believe I deserve it. Before I can figure out how to make this right, she stomps out of the room, and the windows rattle from the slamming front door.

I run my fingers through my beard and stand there for a moment, unreasonably hoping Sami and Lennox didn't somehow hear all of that.

I stride from my bedroom and into the kitchen to grab a bag of frozen veggies out of the freezer. The cold seeps into my skin as I hold it against my eye. Staring out the window, I watch Laney walking down the dirt road toward her house, her strides more than a little angry.

"What was that all about?"

My shoulders stiffen at the sound of Sami's voice, and before I turn around, I drop the bag into the sink. I slowly turn and feel like I'm being sucker punched again, this time in the gut. Looking at Sami, I'm reminded so much of my sister, but my reaction to her, or more accurately, my cock's reaction, is vastly different.

"That depends," I finally say.

Sami arches a brow. "On?"

"On what you heard."

"I heard yelling and the door slamming." She takes a step back and starts to turn around. "Look, I'm gonna get Lennox and we're leaving."

"You can't leave!" I shout, instantly regretting my tone.

Sami whirls back toward me but doesn't come closer. Her cheeks redden, and her fists ball at her sides. "Like hell I can't! I'm not into the whole group thing, and I don't want Lennox exposed to this... *lifestyle*." She sneers the word, and my anger switch flips.

I advance on her. "This lifestyle? What the fuck is wrong with my lifestyle?"

"Nothing." She shrugs. "If you're into that sorta thing." Then she points out the kitchen window. "But I'm pretty sure even your girlfriend has a problem with it. But you refuse to see it."

It takes me a minute to realize what she's thinking but once it clicks, I throw my head back and howl with laughter. I laugh so long my eyes begin to leak, and I have to wipe them in order to see her clearly.

"What's so funny?" she demands, obviously feeling like I'm laughing at her expense.

I suppose I am, but seriously?

"Laney isn't my girlfriend," I tell her when I trust myself enough to speak, and just saying the words out loud causes me to shiver, and not in a good way. "Laney is Shiloh's mom, my sister."

Sami's eyes widen comically, and her shoulders slump. "Oh."

"Oh?" I repeat. "That's all you have to say?"

"I'm sorry."

The words come out sounding more like a question, but I choose to let it go. I take a few more steps toward her until I'm close enough to grip her chin and force her to look me in the eyes.

"Angel, if I had a girlfriend, you and Lennox wouldn't be here. You'd be in one of the other houses. I'm not a fucking saint, but I sure as shit know how to treat a woman and stepping out ain't it."

Sami steps around me and opens the freezer. Ice clinks as she grabs a handful and turns to me. "Do you have a Ziploc bag?"

Her complete shift in conversation throws me off for a moment, but I quickly catch up. I pull open a cupboard door and hand her the box of plastic baggies. Sami plucks one from the opening in the top and shoves the ice inside before sliding the zipper closed.

"Here." She shoves the bag at me. "Put this on your eye. It'll help the swelling."

Before taking what I can only assume is her peace offering, I press two fingers to just below my eye and wince slightly. I take the ice from her and hold it to my face as I did with the frozen veggies.

"Thanks."

"Do you have a first-aid kit?"

"Uh, yeah, in the bathroom."

Sami nods as she pivots on her feet to go toward the bathroom between the guest bedrooms.

"It's down the other hall," I call after her.

Sami switches directions and goes to the other side of the house. When she disappears down the hall, I follow after her, knowing she's not going to find a door other than the one leading to my bedroom.

Standing in the middle of the hall, her head swivels back and forth between the only door and the wall on the opposite side. She glances over her shoulder as if she senses me standing right behind her, and I focus on her facial expressions. They're changing quickly, almost as if a million thoughts are scrambling through her mind and her muscles can't keep up.

"I thought you said there was another bathroom?"

"There is." I lean against the wall just next to my bedroom door. I tilt my head to indicate the room. "It's in there."

Sami takes a deep breath, as if fortifying herself, and then brushes past me. She stalks across the hardwood floor and yanks open the first door she comes to. Seeing that it's the closet, she pushes it shut and moves to the next door. When she pulls that one open, her released breath is audible.

"If you want me to bandage you up, you better get in here."

I take my time joining her in the bathroom, and when images of her in my shower, taking a bubble bath in my tub, naked and wet and fucking sexy as hell, infiltrate my thoughts, I can't stop the grin tugging at my lips. I shake my head to clear it and try to keep as much distance as possible between us.

"It's just a bruise," I say, finally coming to my senses. "No need for bandages and shit."

Sami pulls open a drawer and shuffles through the contents until she finds what she wants. She sets a tube of antibiotic ointment on the counter, as well as a box of assorted Band-aids, before turning to me.

"That cut says otherwise."

Cut?

I lower the bag of ice and lean in toward the mirror to check out my reflection. Sure enough, there's a nasty cut near the corner of my eye, and it's oozing blood. Damn Laney and her stupid rings.

Sami grabs the ice from me and tosses it in the sink before pointing to the closed toilet lid.

"Sit," she demands.

I stare at her in the mirror and arch a brow.

"If you don't want my help, fine. Otherwise, sit down and let me do this for you."

And there's the rub. I don't want or need Sami's help. Especially not to fix me up after my sister of all people punched me. I've had worse done to me… a lot fucking worse, and I've got the scars to prove it. But I *do* want Sami to trust me.

Besides, how fucking bad can it be to let her think she's taking care of me?

SAMI

I try not to look at Snow as he sits down on the toilet seat. In fact, it's all I can do to breathe being in such close proximity to him. I'm embarrassed as hell that I jumped to conclusions earlier. My only defense is the jealousy spiraled out of control when I heard them yelling but couldn't make out all the words. And I've gotta say, the fictitious conversation I created in my head was an argument between lovers, not siblings.

"You're staring."

Snow's voice startles me, and I take a deep breath to center myself and focus on doing what needs done.

"Do you have a washcloth?" I ask, realizing I need something to clean the cut with. "Or peroxide?"

"Washcloths are behind you." Snow tips his head to indicate a shelf housing neatly folded towels. "No peroxide."

I grab a washcloth off the top of the pile and then turn on the faucet to wet it with warm water. I wring it out before gently pressing it to his eye. I expect him to wince and then realize how stupid that expectation is. Snow's a biker, which means he's tougher than most.

"So, you really thought Laney was my girlfriend?" he asks, seemingly needing to fill the silence with small talk.

"Yeah," I admit. "Why would I have thought otherwise?"

"Oh, I don't know," he responds casually. "Maybe because I had just explained about Shiloh and having a sister. Seems girlfriend was a pretty big leap."

I roll my eyes at him and toss the cloth onto the counter. I pick up the Neosporin and put a dab of it straight onto the cut.

"I don't have to explain myself to you," I say hotly and lift the Band-aid box to open it.

"No, you don't. But I feel like you want *me* to explain *myself.*"

I pull out a bandage and peel the wrapper apart, exposing a colorful Spiderman design. The corners of my lips lift.

"You should do that more often," Snow remarks.

"What?" I ask as I affix the Band-aid over the cut.

"Smile."

I immediately school my expression and start cleaning things up, not that there's much to clean. Once the bathroom is back to the way I found it when I walked in, I turn and walk out. Snow follows.

"Where are you going?" he asks.

Without stopping my retreat, or looking at him, I respond with, "I cleaned you up. Now I'm going to go check on my son. Or have you forgotten about him?"

The question is asked with a lot of bitterness because *I* had forgotten about Lennox. For the few minutes I was in that bathroom with Snow, Lennox disappeared from my thoughts because there wasn't room for anything but the swirling confusion about the man who is taking us in and the way he smells, the way he looks, the way he fucking breathes.

Snow's fingers curl around my bicep, and he spins me around, pinning me with his stare. "Of course I didn't forget about Lennox." When I glare at his hand on my arm, he let's go and shoves his fingers through his beard. "And I never asked you to clean me up."

He's right, he didn't. And all that fact does is infuriate me because I did what I always do...I took care of someone who didn't need it, who I have no business taking care of. I blame it on the mom part of my brain.

"Listen," Snow begins. "Why don't you go get Lennox and I'll take you both to my sister's so the two of you can meet? Lennox and Shiloh can play while we're there."

I huff out a laugh. "Pretty sure the woman who slammed your door has no interest in meeting me."

Snow's eyes narrow. "I thought you said you didn't hear anything?"

"I didn't, but you just confirmed it. Whatever the hell the two of you were yelling about had to do with me and my son. So forgive me if I'm not jumping at the chance to go to her house."

Snow shakes his head. "We didn't argue about you." When I give him a skeptical look, he caves. "Fine, we did, but it wasn't really about *you* specifically. She's just protective of Shiloh and has some concerns about strangers being at the compound."

"You don't have to explain. Trust me, as a mother, I get it."

Snow sighs as if hearing those words lifts the weight of the world off him.

"I said I get it. I didn't say I was going to her house or that I'm not getting my son and leaving."

I turn away from him and walk the rest of the way to the guest room, slowly opening the door when I reach it. When I left Lennox earlier, he was curled up on the bed, fast asleep, the stress of the last day or two finally catching up to his little body.

When the door is open enough for me to see he's still

asleep, I back up and pull the door closed. Leaning my forehead against it, I take a few deep breaths.

"Sami," Snow says from behind me as he rests his hand on my back. "Laney will come around, I promise. She's just... she's had a rough few years. Hell, we all have. But please don't leave because of her. Where will you and Lennox go?"

Tears prick the back of my eyes because I can't answer that question. We could go to a shelter, but that's not where I want my son to grow up. I could try to talk to Corey and see if he'll let us come home, but I simply don't want to. He may be Lennox's dad, but he's not a good man. He's not even close to being a good person.

"Sami?" Snow prods.

"Fine," I mumble.

"You'll stay?"

"Yes." I straighten and turn to face him. "But only until I can figure out a better option."

Snow lifts his hands as he takes a step back. "That works. I do have one question though."

"What?"

"What happens when you don't find a better option?"

"I will."

"Maybe," he concedes. "But ya know what they say?"

"What do they say?"

"The grass isn't always greener on the other side."

"Trust me, I'm well aware of that."

I push past Snow and go into his living room, where I flop down onto his couch.

"One more question," he says, sitting next to me.

"What?" I ask through gritted teeth.

"What happens when you realize you actually want to stay?"

"Not happening," I scoff.

Snow kicks his feet up onto the coffee table, relaxing like he owns the place. Oh wait, he does.

"We'll see about that."

SNOW

"*A*re we gonna get started anytime soon?

I lift my tumbler to my lips and down the rest of my bourbon while remaining focused on the snow flying outside the window. In the five hours since I drove Sami and Lennox onto the property, mother nature has put down almost a foot of white powder so even if she wanted to leave, she can't. Not that my truck wouldn't easily plow through it, but she doesn't need to know that.

"Pres?"

Ice clinks against the sides of the glass as I turn around and stare at Dip.

"What?" I snap.

"We getting started soon?" he repeats, unnecessarily. I heard him the first time.

I walk to the table and set down my empty glass before focusing on the members who are present. I called the meeting on an emergency basis, although I'm sure they won't see this as an emergency.

"You got somewhere better to be?" I arch a brow at my Road Captain.

"Somewhere better than stuck in this room with a bunch of jackasses?" Dip asks. "Yeah, I do. But you said this was an emergency, so here I am."

Anger hits me hard. There is nothing more important than Satan's Legacy... *nothing*. And the idea that one of my higher-ranking members thinks there is, poses a problem.

"Dude, shut the fuck up before you cease to exist," Duck snarls. "I don't give a shit if you've got the goddamn Queen of England's pussy waiting on you, it's not more important than this."

"We don't even know what *this* is?" Dip counters.

"What the patch binds together, let no force tear apart. Satan's Legacy now and forever." I narrow my eyes at Dip. "Ring any bells?"

Dip raises his hands in surrender before dropping into his usual chair. "That's exactly what I'm trying to live up to," he argues, a little calmer, and then turns his attention to Duck. "It's not pussy I need to get to, or are you forgetting we have a drop tonight with Corey?"

Motherfucker!

I did forget... sort of. My head is so wrapped around Sami and the way her touch felt when she was cleaning the cut on my face, on her expression when she talked about wanting to leave, the jealousy that swam in her eyes after Laney stormed out. Oh, and let's not forget the way the bedroom door slammed after Sami left me sitting on the couch pondering all the ways I could make her want to stay with me.

"Of course I didn't forget," I say instead. "But I wanted to discuss one more thing with you before it was time to leave."

"You don't have to explain yourself, Pres," Duck states.

"Apparently I do." I motion for everyone to sit, and they do. "I'll make this quick." I wait for interruptions, but when there are none, I continue. "We have the drop with Corey tonight, as Dip so unnecessarily pointed out. But we've got two other things to discuss. Before I move on to the others, any last-minute questions about tonight?"

A chorus of 'no's fill the room.

"Good. Moving on."

"Is this about Laney?" Magic asks, and I sharpen my focus on him.

"What makes you think that?"

Magic shrugs. "No reason, unless the way she was stomping through the snow earlier is cause for concern. Dude, she was pissed about something."

"As a matter of fact, she was." I sigh. "She is. But she'll get over it."

"If it's something she'll get over, why do we need to discuss it?" Duck asks.

For a moment, I consider backtracking, pretending that the problem doesn't exist, and that Laney's life is hers and hers alone. But I quickly dismiss that idea because growing up in the Satan's Legacy, she's well aware that her life is not hers alone and club members sometimes need to know what the fuck is going on.

I take a deep breath and slowly release it. "Laney isn't exactly thrilled about Sami and Lennox being on the property," I admit.

"You really thought she would be?" Magic asks.

"I think it doesn't matter what she thinks because she doesn't get a fucking say in what happens with the club," I bark.

"Bro," Duck interjects. "Laney isn't a club member. And you're right, she doesn't get a say in club business, but we also don't get a say in her life."

I shake my head as if doing so will make it untrue.

"Do you really blame her after everything that went down

with Cedric?" Magic asks. "She tries to put on a good front, but she's nowhere near over it."

"And you know this how?" I ask, my hackles raising over the fact that he seems to know more about my own sister than I do.

Magic stands and leans on the table, a scowl on his face. "I know this because I pay attention," he snarls. "It's not hard to figure out, Snow."

"And what have you seen that I haven't?"

Magic sits back down. "Nothing, forget it."

"No, I'm not gonna forget it!" I pound my fists on the table. "Fucking explain!"

"Snow, man, your sister is constantly looking over her shoulder," Duck says, no doubt sensing I'm dangerously close to launching myself over the table at Magic. "She home-schools Shiloh, and he's not allowed to play with kids outside of the club. She hasn't been on a date in—"

"I get it,' I grumble, not needing to hear more. "Jesus, this sucks."

"It does," Magic agrees, the first thing we've seen eye to eye on since entering this room. "But it'll pass. It hasn't been all that long."

"It's been two years," I remind him. "When will she get it that she's safe here? Fuck, she's safe everywhere... Cedric's dead."

"Yeah, he is, but that doesn't change anything for her."

"Uh, I hate to break up a good argument, but why did we have to meet about this?" Toga asks, speaking up for the first time.

"I need extra security on Laney." Before anyone can protest, I hold up a hand. "I am well aware that Laney isn't going to be happy about it, but I don't care. I may not think there's a threat to her, but she does."

"So, what, you want us to protect her without her knowledge?" Magic asks.

"No. The whole point of this is so she knows. I want her to feel safe. I don't think for a second that Sami and Lennox pose a threat to her, but I'd be fucking stupid if I ignored the possibility that things with Corey could get ugly. He's not the brightest bulb, but he's about to learn he's public enemy number one to Satan's Legacy so who knows what will happen?"

"I can see if Laney wants one of us to stay with her and Shiloh," Magic offers.

"No." I quickly dismiss that suggestion with a shake of my head. "I want her to feel safe, not smothered. Get some of the prospects to do 24/7 patrol around her house and the perimeter of the property. That should make her feel better."

Magic's shoulders deflate, but I ignore it. He's just being pissy because he didn't get his way. Too damn bad. This isn't about him.

"What's the other thing you needed to talk about?" Duck asks, reminding me that Laney's fear isn't the only reason I called this impromptu emergency meeting.

"The toy drive and Christmas Carnival," I say, and everyone's eyes light up. "The toy drive has already started, but I need someone to make the rounds and pick up what's there. And the carnival is in two weeks, so we really need to get on it."

"Uh, Pres," Toga begins. "There's not much left to do for it. We've got all the vendors lined up, contracts signed, volunteers set up with their schedules, and we've been pushing it like crazy on social media."

"And what about the tree?" I ask. "We have that yet?"

Toga and Magic exchange a look. They're the two who usually take care of that, with the help of Laney and Shiloh, as well as other member's kids, and when possible, families from the shelter.

"I'll take the lack of answer as a no." I stroke my beard. "Go ahead and see if there are any families from the shelter who want to help decorate the tree once we secure it, but other than that, I'll handle everything else."

"Let me guess…" Duck chuckles. "A certain mama and her son are going to be going with you to the tree farm?"

"Got a problem with that?" I snap at him before shifting my gaze to the other brothers, practically daring them to argue.

"No problem," Duck says. "But what about Laney and Shiloh? Little man is gonna be upset if he's left out."

"You seriously think I'm going to disappoint my nephew?"

"Normally, no. But I'm not so sure you're thinking clearly right now."

Duck is the only person who can get away with saying shit like that, but saying it in front of my men? Unacceptable. I reach across the corner of the table and wrap my fingers around his throat.

"Wanna say that again?" I snarl.

Duck shakes his head. I shove him so hard his weight topples his chair to the floor. The others smirk but don't dare let out a laugh. Duck scrambles to his feet and glares at me. He opens and closes his mouth several times but wisely chooses to remain silent.

I turn to face the others. "Get the fuck out of here and do the run." I focus on Magic. "Report back when it's done."

Magic, Toga, Dip, and a few others rile out of the room. Duck remains behind, fuming.

"Did you need something else?" I ask as I walk to the bar to pour myself another drink.

"That was uncalled for, and you know it."

Once my glass is full, I take a swig before turning to face him.

"Don't ever put me in the position to have to do it again," I grit out. "You may be my best friend, but in this room, you're the VP, and that means I outrank you."

"And that's the problem," he snaps back. "You're making a distinction. I can be both your best friend and VP. They aren't mutually exclusive. Especially when the shit a friend would call you out on is shit that also impacts the club."

"Sami and Lennox being here does not impact the club!" I shout, reaching my limit.

Duck shakes his head and walks to the door. Before leaving the room, he glances over his shoulder with a disappointed expression.

"Keep telling yourself that... *Pres.*"

SAMI

"*M*om?"

I roll to my side and curl my arms under my head as I stare at Lennox. It's the middle of the night and I have yet to fall asleep. I keep trying to convince myself it's because I'm in a new place and all the creeks and sounds are freaking me out, but even I know that's not true. I'm awake because I'm waiting for Snow to come home.

"Yeah, baby?"

"I wanna go home," he whines. "This was supposed to be fun, but I haven't even been able to play with Sh-sh—"

"Shiloh," I supply the name for him.

"Yeah," Lennox says with enthusiasm. "Shiloh. I thought I was gonna get to play with him."

I think back over the argument between Snow and Laney. I don't really know the details, but Snow confirmed she's wary of us being here. I won't tell Lennox that though, or about the fact that Snow offered to take us over so the two boys could play, and I refused.

"Well, baby, I think they're all just really busy. Maybe tomorrow."

I reach across the double bed to ruffle his hair, but he pulls away. Maybe I should have slept in the other guest room. But I couldn't quite bring myself to be away from Lennox in case he needed me. Although he never seems to need me much anymore.

"But he said if I was good, I could pick something fun to do." Lennox sits up, pulling the covers off me as he does. "He lied."

I heave a sigh and sit up. "He didn't lie," I tell him, although I want to agree with him because it pisses me off that Snow got my son's hopes up for nothing. "But maybe he's planning something really big as a surprise."

And now I have to figure something out because if there's not a 'really big surprise' for Lennox, he's gonna think I'm a liar. Which I am, I guess.

"Your mama's right."

Snow's deep rumble has both Lennox and I turning toward the door. I know I closed it when I came in here, but somehow, Snow managed to open it without me even hearing. Some protective mom I am.

The hall light is on—I missed that, too?—and Snow's broad shoulders fill the doorway. I swallow past the lump in my throat seeing him causes. There's no denying he's attractive, very much so, but that doesn't matter. There was a time I thought Corey was cute too.

"You lied to me," Lennox accuses before I can get a word out.

Snow crosses the room and skirts the bed to sit on the edge of the mattress next to Lennox. He doesn't seem to let my son's glower bother him. In fact, he appears to be holding back a laugh.

"I know it seems that way," Snow says. "But I didn't lie."

"But you said—"

"I know what I said. But your mama's right. I was just

trying to surprise you with something that's gonna be so much fun you're not gonna know how to handle it."

Lennox sighs with pure little boy exasperation. Now *I'm* trying not to laugh.

"I don't believe you."

Snow shrugs. "That's fine because there won't be a surprise if you keep giving your mama and me a hard time," he says casually. "Remember when I told you that, as long as you're here, you need to show respect to all adults?"

Lennox's gaze darts to me then back to Snow, his face falling because he knows he can't argue anymore.

"Yeah."

"Good. Now, get some sleep and, in the morning, after both you and your mom have gotten some rest, we'll re-evaluate. Sound fair?"

"What's re-evaluate mean?"

"It means we'll see how things are going at that time, and if you're behaving with respect, we'll discuss the surprise I was planning."

Lennox quickly lays down and pulls the covers up to his chin. Snow and I are no longer able to hold in our laughter.

"Night," Snow says before standing.

He locks eyes with me and nods toward the door as if asking me to join him in the hall. I kiss Lennox on the forehead before leaving him to hopefully fall back to sleep.

"Leave the hall light on?" Lennox asks just before I step through the door. "Please," he tacks on.

"You got it. Love you."

I pull the door so it stays open a crack. Lennox's mumbled 'love you too' reaches my ears, and I smile as I walk down the hall to see Snow in the living room. He's standing there, feet braced apart, hands in his pocket, and a regretful look on his face.

"Sorry I was gone so long," he says. "I really didn't mean to be."

"You don't need to apologize. You can come and go as you please. It's your house. We're the interlopers here."

"No, you're not." He rushes forward and rests his hands on my shoulders. "I told you, I want you to treat this like your home."

"Because you think we're gonna end up staying?"

Snow heaves a sigh. "No. Because it seems you and Lennox need some stability and you're welcome here as long as you want to be here. I don't want you to feel like you have to walk on pins and needles because this isn't technically your house."

"That sounds like you still think we're gonna stay."

"Look, I'm not going to sugar coat things, okay?"

"I prefer it that way."

He gives a curt nod. "Tonight with Corey went exactly as planned, which is good, but…"

My heart drops and my mind races with just what it would take to leave here with Lennox in tow and be safe. Somehow sensing my panic, Snow's grip on my shoulders shifts so he's pulling me toward him.

"But that means things are about to get dangerous. For you, for Lennox, for all of us. So why not stay here, where you know you'll be safe, for however long that takes? Once the danger passes, you and Lennox can leave. I've said that from the beginning, and I meant it."

Safe. What does that even mean? There was a time I thought I knew, but over time and with experience, I realized the meaning changes. Sometimes safety is being with someone who you love and who loves you back, other times the meaning is much more basic. This is one of those other times.

Right now, all I need to feel safe is a roof over my and my

son's heads, clothes on our back, and the knowledge that we don't have to scrounge through dumpsters for food. Safety means staying here, with Snow and Satan's Legacy, for an undetermined amount of time.

I push away from him and lift my chin so I can meet his eyes.

"Okay. We'll stay."

SNOW

*B*read pops up from the toaster just as I flip the omelet I'm making for Sami. I wasn't sure what Lennox would want for breakfast so I texted Laney earlier this morning and asked her if I could have one of her many boxes of kid-approved cereal. She agreed but didn't even bother coming in when she dropped it off, choosing to set it on the porch and text me that it was there instead.

I slather butter onto the toast and drop it on the waiting plate. When the omelet is done, I add it with the toast. As I move the table, Sami walks into the kitchen, rubbing her eyes as if to rid them of sleep.

"Morning," I say, setting down her breakfast.

"Hmm," she grumbles.

"So, not a morning person." I chuckle. "I'll remember that."

Sami glances at the food I prepared and then shifts her eyes to me. "I don't do breakfast."

"Good thing it's not for you, then," I say, hoping she doesn't catch the disappointment in my tone, even though she did nothing to hide the lie in hers.

"Yeah, good thing."

I turn to lift the box of Froot Loops with marshmallows off the counter and show them to her. "Does Lennox do breakfast?"

A hint of a smile appears on her lips, but she quickly masks it. "Sometimes. When we have something he likes."

I shake the box. "Does he like this? Laney brought it, so I hope so."

Sami nods.

I grab a bowl from the cupboard and pour some cereal into it. I don't bother with the milk because I don't want it to get soggy before Lennox wakes up.

Sami sits down at the table. "How'd you convince your sister to be okay with us here?"

I turn my back on her, my mind scrambling to come up with a response that doesn't sound like bullshit. Because, let's face it, unless I'm honest, it's going to be bullshit.

"Oh, that," I begin. "We talked last night. It's all good." I grab a knife and fork out of the drawer and return to the table. "We'll head over there later, if that's okay with you."

"Yeah, sure." Her eyes fall to the omelet. "Lennox would enjoy that."

"I can make another one if you're hungry," I offer nonchalantly. "I know you said you don't do breakfast but ya gotta eat."

She waves her hand dismissively. "I'm fine. I usually just grab a few slices of bacon before starting my shift at the diner."

"I got bacon in the fridge," I say, hitching my thumb over my shoulder. "Wouldn't take long to fry some up."

The tip of Sami's tongue darts out to lick her bottom lip and my cock tries to tear through my sweats. She continues to stare at the food, and I don't dare move my gaze away from her mouth.

"Moooooom!"

Lennox's shout cuts through the tension, which I'm sure only I feel, and Sami hops up from her chair to rush from the kitchen.

"Coming," she calls out to him.

No, you're not. But you will be if I have anything to say about it.

A few minutes later, after I've consumed half of the omelet, Sami returns with her son, and she instructs him to sit at the table.

"Morning," I say to him.

"Hmm."

Oh dear God, he's just like his mother.

Sami opens the fridge and grabs the milk, then she begins opening and closing drawers until she finds the silverware and a spoon. She returns to the table to pour the liquid over Lennox's cereal.

"Thanks," he mumbles when she hands him the spoon.

"You're welcome."

I finish the omelet while Lennox digs into his cereal. He's quiet until about half the bowl is gone, then he swipes his mouth with the back of his hand and lifts his head to look in my direction.

"You said we'd revaluate in the morning if I'm being good," he reminds me.

"Re-evaluate," I correct him as I chuckle. "And, yes, I did."

"Am I being good?"

"Lennox, finish your breakfast and then we'll talk," Sami instructs.

Lennox sighs but does as he's told. He finishes his cereal and slurps the remaining milk. "'Kay, I'm done."

"Please rinse your bowl out in the sink."

Lennox darts his eyes from me to his mom and back again, almost as if waiting for Sami to step in and not allow me to tell her son what to do. She doesn't. Lennox hops off his chair and carries his dishes to the sink. He has to stand on his tiptoes to reach the faucet and I make a mental note to get a step stool for him.

While Lennox is busy doing that, I take a moment to finish the conversation I was having with Sami.

"Do you want me to make some of the bacon in the fridge?" I ask her.

Lennox swivels his head and grins. "I want bacon!" He pumps his fist in the air. "I love bacon!"

"Lennox, you already—"

"It's fine," I say quickly. "If he's still hungry, why not let him have some?"

Sami glares at me but realizing she has the full attention of her son, she quickly schools her features and smiles.

"Fine," she caves. "But I'll make it for him."

"And what about you?"

"I'm not hun—"

"Angel, you were staring at that omelet like you were trying to will it into your stomach. If you're hungry, eat."

"She never eats until she goes to work," Lennox says, causing Sami's cheeks to redden. "There's usually only enough for me and Dad."

"Lennox!" Sami admonishes. "That's enough. Go change out of your pjs and brush your teeth."

"But he said I could have some bacon," Lennox counters. "And that we'd talk about what fun things we're gonna do."

"Listen to your mama," I tell the boy as I stand and carry my plate to the sink. "When you come back out, we'll talk."

Lennox huffs but stomps out of the kitchen, presumably to change and brush his teeth. I try hard not to laugh because he seriously needs to work on his manners but right now, he's just being a typical kid. He reminds me so much of Shiloh.

"I was handling it," Sami snaps when a door closes down the hall.

I open the fridge and pull out the package of bacon. "Didn't think you weren't."

"If you really want us to stay here, you need to let me parent him."

I throw some bacon into the frying pan I used for the omelet and turn on the burner. "I am letting you parent him."

"No, you weren't." She steps up next to me and crosses her arms over her chest. "What're you doing?"

"Making bacon."

"I can see that," she snaps. "But why?"

The meat sizzles in the pan and I flip it before glancing at her. "Because you need to eat, and he wanted some bacon."

Something resembling a growl escapes past her lips. "Why are you doing this?"

"Pretty sure I just told you... because you need to eat a—"

"No, not that. Why are you helping us?"

"Oh."

The bacon is fully cooked, and I place a paper towel on a plate to spread the bacon on to cool.

"That's it? That's all you've got to say? Just 'oh'?"

I scoot the grease filled pan to the back burner and turn the stove off before turning to fully face Sami. I lean my hip against the counter and mimic her pose by crossing my arms over my chest.

"No, that's not it. I'm helping you because you need it. If you'll recall, I gave you some quarters and walked away. Dammit, I didn't force you to use them, but you did. Now you're here and while you are more than welcome to leave any time you want, I'd strongly advise against it."

"Why, because Corey's dangerous?" she huffs. "How do I know you're not?"

"He is, and you don't."

"At least with him I know what to expect."

"Seems to me you had no fucking clue what to expect with him," I snarl. "Or are you forgetting that there was plenty of info you didn't know?"

"Of course not." Her arms drop to her sides, slapping against her thighs. "How could I forget that he's some sort of drug criminal and apparently I had no idea?"

A door in the hallway opens and footsteps sound on the hardwood until Lennox appears in the kitchen. He spots the plate of bacon and makes a beeline for it.

"We'll finish this discussion later," Sami whispers harshly.

"Looking forward to it."

We both turn to focus on Lennox. He only eats two pieces before handing the plate to his mom. When he wipes his mouth clean on his sleeve, he focuses on me.

"So, now can we valuate things?"

SAMI

"*S*he doesn't bite, I promise."

Snow's words do nothing to lessen the anxiety I feel racing through my veins as we walk to his sister's house. Lennox, on the other hand, laughs. We keep walking, trudging through the snow, and I ball my hands into fists in my jacket pockets. Correction, Snow's jackets. Snow offered to drive but I refused, choosing instead to let Lennox burn off some of his energy before we get there with the hope that he'll be more likely to be on his best behavior.

"It's just up ahead," Snow says as he points at a house beyond a line of trees.

The house is different from Snow's, different from any of the others we've passed. It's clear a woman lives there. Christmas lights adorn the porch, bright and colorful. There are Christmas decorations in the yard and lighted netting draped over bushes. It's beautiful and not at all what I expected.

Just as we reach the porch, the front door swings open and a man steps out. He's not wearing a cut like the other bikers, so I assume he's Laney's boyfriend with the sheepish look he shoots Snow.

"Magic, what are you doing here?"

"Just checking in on Laney," he answers. "You said you wanted security beefed up."

"I also said I didn't want it shoved in her face."

"Sorry, Pres. Just trying to get the ball rolling. Everyone is so busy with all the holiday festivities coming up, I figured a quick pop in wouldn't hurt." He grins. "Besides, I told her I was here to talk about the carnival so no worries."

"Fine," Snow snaps. He glances at me quickly before returning his attention back to Magic. "I'll meet you at the clubhouse later to discuss some business."

"You got it." Magic jogs down the steps and turns around so he's walking backward away from the porch. "I assume you're Sami, ma'am. And that's your son, Lennox? Snow isn't the best with manners."

"Jesus," Snow mutters. "Sami, this is Magic, our Enforcer and a pain in my ass. Magic, this is Sami and Lennox."

Magic throws his head back and laughs and for the first time since I stepped out of Snow's house, some of my tension eases.

"It's nice to meet you, Magic."

"You too, Sami." He steps forward, back toward us, and sticks out his hand. "And you too, Lennox."

Lennox shakes Magic's hand.

"Damn, that's some grip you got there, son."

Uh oh.

Lennox's demeanor shifts so fast you'd miss it if you blinked. "I'm not your son!"

"No, you're not." Magic grins. "But you should probably get used to being called that by a lot of the guys here. It's just how we roll."

Lennox narrows his eyes as if considering this and then shrugs. "Okay."

Snow and I exchange a look, both fully aware that that could have gone very differently. Hell, it did when Snow made the same mistake.

"Anyway, things to do and people to see," Magic says. "I'll catch ya later."

With that, he turns and disappears down the road, toward the main house.

"Why does security need beefed up?" I ask Snow.

He tips his head toward Lennox, who is kneeling in the snow next to the porch. "Can we talk about that a little later?"

As much as I want to demand we discuss it now, I don't want Lennox scared. And the fact that Snow takes my son into consideration does something funny to me.

"Yeah."

Snow nods and climbs the steps. Lennox and I follow. Rather than knocking, Snow twists the knob and pushes open the door before stepping inside.

"Laney!" he calls out.

"Be right there," she yells from somewhere in the house.

Shiloh comes barreling down the steps and launches himself at Snow.

"Uncle Zeke!" he shouts as Snow catches him.

"Hey buddy."

Shiloh looks at Lennox and then grins at his uncle. "Finally," he says dramatically. "I didn't think you were ever gonna bring him to play with me."

Snow sets him back on his feet and ruffles his hair. "Sorry, dude. Things got a little hectic."

"You mean mom got mad at you and wou—"

"Shiloh!" a woman snaps from the top of the steps. "We have company."

Shiloh rolls his eyes. "Duh, mom."

"Don't start with me, Shi."

"Sorry," he says.

Laney walks down the steps, running her fingers through her damp hair as she does. Snow watches her, an odd look crossing his face.

"Passed Magic when we got here," he says casually.

"Oh, yeah," she says and stops in front of us. "The fact that he was here just proves the point I was trying to make yesterday."

"Laney, not the time or place," Snow warns.

"You brought it up."

Snow heaves a sigh and looks at me. "Sami, this is my bratty little sister, Laney." He swivels his head toward her. "Laney, this is Sami and her son Lennox."

Laney's expression instantly warms, although it seems more forced than natural. "Nice to meet you both."

"You too." I fidget with my hands in my pockets. "Um, if this isn't a good time, we can leave. I don't want to burden anyone."

Snow glares at his sister until her shoulders sag.

"You're not burdening anyone, Sami," Laney says. "I promise. I just have some…" She glances at the boys and lowers her voice. "… PTSD from shit and I didn't mean to make you feel bad or anything."

Before I can say anything, Snow corrals the kids.

"Shiloh, why don't you take Lennox to your room and you guys can play until it's time to leave?"

"Where are we going, Uncle Zeke?"

"Yeah, *Uncle Zeke*, where are we going?" Laney parrots.

"He won't tell you," Lennox pipes up. "He's been telling me there's a surprise all morning and so far, he won't give up any information."

"Just go," Snow chuckles.

Shiloh and Lennox race up the steps, both talking a mile a minute, but I can't make out a word they're saying in their excitement.

"Door open, Shi," Laney calls after them.

"I know, I know."

When the boys are no longer in ear shot, Laney turns toward Snow. "Now, what the hell do you have up your sleeve?"

"I'd like to know the answer to that too," I say.

Snow's head falls back, and he stares at the ceiling. "Motherfucker, what have I done?"

"Look," Laney begins. "You brought her here so don't get pissed at us when we actually become friends and gang up on you. It'll be your fault."

"Ya know what?" I say, grinning at Snow. "I think I'm gonna like your sister."

Snow lowers his gaze to me and then shifts it to Laney. "Not even twenty-four hours ago you were giving me hell for inviting them to stay. What the fuck has changed?"

Laney scowls and turns on her heel to walk away toward the kitchen. "You're an ass, Zeke," she says over her shoulder.

He strides after her and I'm left standing just inside the doorway like an idiot. When he twists his head to look back, I quick-step to catch up to them.

"Sami, can I get you anything to drink? I've got coffee, water, juice boxes..." She pauses and smirks. "I've also got some Kahlua if you need some fortification to get through the day with my dumb-ass brother."

"Watch it," Snow warns. "I'm not in the mood for your shit today."

Laney cocks her hip and rests her hand on it. "Really? *You're* not in the mood? You didn't seem to have any problem bringing shit up a minute ago."

Their arguing is making me more nervous than I already

was, so I step between them. "Look, I don't want to cause problems. Seriously, we can just go home. We'll be fine."

"To Corey?" Laney asks.

I dart my eyes between the siblings and settle my look on Laney. "Uh, yeah." My words sound more like a question than an answer.

"Yeah, not happening," she says. "He's a fucking douchebag."

"Laney!" Snow admonishes, almost like she did with Shiloh earlier. "He's Lennox's dad."

"And look how well that turned out for me!" Laney shouts.

"Wait, what?" I snap. "Corey is Shilo—"

"No," Laney insists. "All I mean is, I know what it's like to have someone like Corey as the father of my child and it can't possibly be a good thing."

"Trust me," I say. "I'm aware of how bad for Lennox Corey is. But Corey is his father and Lennox loves him. I don't know how to get around that."

"Let me worry about that," Snow says vehemently.

"Oh, right, cause what are you gonna do? Kill him?" I chuckle because I'm nowhere near serious, but the look on his face tells me I should be. I shake my head. "No, no. You can't... I can't let..." I continue shaking my head. "You're not seriously gonna kill him, are you?"

"Not necessarily," Snow says as he shrugs.

"Oh my God," I mumble and start to walk backward, away from him, away from this. "This is insane."

"Sami, stop," Snow demands.

And I freaking do!

He closes the distance between us, but Laney stays back, taking in the scene. Snow lifts my hands in his and when I try to tug mine free, he tightens his grip.

"Angel, I would *never* do anything to hurt you or Lennox."

His eyes are intense, imploring me to believe the words spilling from his lips. "I couldn't. I may not be the epitome of a good man, but when it comes to people I care about, all they get is the good parts of me."

"How can you say you care about me?" I argue, wanting to believe him but having trouble wrapping my head around it. "You barely know me."

"He cares about you because you're nothing like our mother," Laney says before Snow can answer.

I look past Snow at his sister and see her walking toward us. When she stops next to him, she says, "She was a piece of shit. Didn't care about us or our father or this club. She tried to take us once. Got a few states away and ran out of money so she plopped us in a shelter while she did whatever it was she had to in order to survive. Our dad found us a few weeks later and brought us home."

Snow drops my hands and strokes his beard. He's looking at me but it's as if I'm not even here, like he's focused on something so far away he can barely see it.

"Sami, I'm sorry we got into it in front of you," Laney says when her brother remains quiet. "Me not wanting you and Lennox here had nothing to do with you and everything to do with my own crap." She looks up at her brother quickly and then back to me. "But my brother's different around you. Even in the few minutes I've seen you together this morning, that's pretty clear. I think you and Lennox are exactly what he needs." She takes a deep breath. "And maybe, *just maybe*, he's exactly what you need."

"I… I don't know what to say to that."

"Nothing." Snow finally seems to have rejoined the present and forces a smile. "Now, who's ready for some fun?"

Laney looks at me and gives a slight shake of her head as if to say 'just go with it'.

"I know I am," she tells him. "Apparently, you've been

talking to Lennox about some surprise for a while, so I know the boys are."

"Shiloh, Lennox!" Snow shouts. "Come here."

As if they were waiting in the doorway, they race down the stairs and skid to a stop in front of us so fast, there's barely time to blink.

Snow claps his hands and rubs them together. "Who's ready for an adventure?"

Both boys jump up and down yelling 'I am, I am'.

"You still haven't told us what we're doing, where we're going," I remind him.

Snow glances around the house, which is open concept, before settling his gaze on the beautifully decorated Christmas tree in the living room.

"I need one of those," he says as he tilts his head toward the tree.

"You're gonna get a Christmas tree?" Laney asks as if it's an insane concept.

"Yeah," he says. "I haven't had one in a while, and I think it's about time I put one up."

"You've never had one," Laney states. "Like, not once since you moved into that house."

"I never saw the point," he argues. "I was always here Christmas morning."

I listen to their exchange while watching Lennox's reaction. We can relate to Snow. We haven't had a tree in years. Corey always thought it was a frivolous expense, even when I found a fake one at a thrift shop for under twenty-five bucks. And Christmas presents? Other than the one or two I could afford to get with my tips from the diner, there weren't any. Any money left over after bills, Corey took and did God knows what with.

You now know where that money went.

"I think getting a tree sounds like fun," I say, resting my hand on Snow's arm without thinking.

"Are we gonna go to Walmart to get one?" Lennox asks.

"Walmart?" Snow repeats. "No, we're going to a tree farm to cut down our own and then we'll bring it home to decorate."

"Do you even have ornaments?" Laney asks.

"Okay," Snow says on a sigh. "We *are* going to Walmart, but only to get ornaments. We're still getting the damn tree at the tree farm."

SNOW

"I had fun today."

I carry Shiloh to Laney's truck and put him in the passenger seat before buckling his seatbelt. I turn toward my sister, who is behind me.

"Me too."

"Your nephew definitely had a blast. I think all the fresh air wore him out though. He'll sleep good tonight."

"Glad I could help."

"Are you sure you don't want us to stay and help decorate?" Laney asks.

Part of me wants my sister and nephew to be here, to be buffers in the awkward moments, but the bigger part of me wants to have this experience with only Sami and Lennox.

"Nah, I've got this."

Laney grins. "I'm sure you do."

"Ya know, for someone who was so opposed to my guests, you sure don't seem to have a problem with them now."

Laney lifts a shoulder. "Eh, she's great. And Lennox? He's a handful and has an attitude at times but I have no doubt it's because of Corey. Sami is too good a mother to have it come from her."

I scowl, remembering that I still have to meet with Magic and the others about Corey. "Yeah, well, hopefully Corey won't be an issue for long."

"I don't even want to know."

"Even if you did, you know I wouldn't tell you." I glance over my shoulder at my house. "I better get back inside and kick off the decorating festivities. I still have a meeting tonight and can't be late, but I don't want to rush the fun for Sami and Lennox."

Laney pats me on the arm. "Go have fun, big brother."

I chuckle and shake my head. "I love you, ya know?"

"I know." She walks around to the driver's side and opens the door. Before getting in, she says, "I love you too."

I watch as she pulls away toward her house. When she disappears around the curve, I trudge up the walkway and inside my own home.

"They didn't have to leave," Sami says as I stomp the snow off my boots.

"No, but Laney wanted to get Shiloh home so he could get some of his school work done."

"Holy shit!"

"What?" I arch a brow at Sami.

"With everything going on, I totally forgot about school. Christmas break doesn't start for another two weeks."

I glance at Lennox, who is busy emptying bag after bag of all the decorations we bought onto the floor. I assure myself that he's so busy I can't speak freely and not worry he'll overhear.

"I actually talked to Laney about that," I tell Sami. "She homeschools Shiloh and she said she'd be more than happy to have Lennox join them."

"I can't do that to her," she counters as she glances at her son. "Besides, he's already losing so much, I can't take his friends away from him too."

"I get it," I say. "But I need you to understand that it's not safe for Lennox to go to school right now. It would be better if he's here, on the compound, where we know we can keep him safe. And he won't miss any of his education."

"Why isn't he safe at school?"

"I can't get into the details," I tell her, knowing it's not the answer she wants. "Angel, it's club business and I can't talk about club business. What I will tell you is Corey's already angry and unpredictable, and that's only going to get worse over the next few weeks."

"Snow, I can't do secrets. Not after everything. I just... can't. Either you tell me what's happening or I'm taking my son and we're out of here."

"Hey, guys," Lennox interrupts from his spot on the floor. "Are we gonna decorate or what?"

Sami and I share a look, one that almost seems like we're daring each other to be the one who kills Lennox's fun.

"Yeah, baby," she finally looks at him and says. "We're gonna decorate." She returns her gaze to me. "This conversation isn't finished."

"Understood." I turn away from her and focus on the task that was supposed to make this day extra special. "Ready to put the lights on the tree, bud?"

"What about the ornaments?" Lennox asks, holding up several in his hands.

"Well, we need to put the lights on first, because it'll be harder to do if the ornaments are already on the tree," I explain.

We bought an eight-foot tree, so I made sure we also got plenty of lights. Since they're new and have yet to get in that Christmas tangle, it doesn't take us long to get them on the tree.

"Is there a certain way to put the ornaments on?" Lennox asks before hanging the first one.

The question takes me by surprise and Sami's expression turns sad and... ashamed? I have a feeling that neither of them have decorated many Christmas trees and as for Lennox, I can understand, but for Sami? It makes me want to learn more about her childhood.

"Nope," I tell Lennox. "Just grab an ornament and hang them on the tree. Try to space them out enough that it doesn't look overcrowded but also try to make sure there aren't any noticeable gaps."

"So, yes, there is a certain way?" he counters.

I throw my head back and laugh. "Yeah, I suppose there kind of is. Basically, just have fun."

"I can do that."

Sami and I stand back and watch Lennox go to town on the ornaments. He starts at the bottom, where it's easiest for him to reach and when he hits a height that's too high, he looks over his shoulder expectantly.

"Need help, baby?" Sami asks.

Lennox looks at his mom and then at me before nodding. "Snow, think you can lift me up?"

Surprised by the request, I stay rooted in place for a moment, almost as if waiting on Sami to stop me from agreeing. When she doesn't, I step toward Lennox and the tree.

"How ya wanna do this, little man?" I ask. "Want me to lift you up or wanna sit on my shoulders?"

"Shoulders!"

I bend to lift him up and put him on my shoulders. He's way too tall to get the middle of the tree now but maybe he can do the topper. As if she reads my mind, Sami hands me the light up star we bought earlier.

"Shouldn't this go on last?" Lennox asks.

"Nah, doesn't matter when we put it on," I say. "As long as

it goes on. We can wait to plug it in if you want, so it's lit up last."

His little body shakes on my shoulders, and I assume it's because he's nodding.

Sami starts putting ornaments around the middle of the tree and handing Lennox other ones to put up top. The tree is completely decorated within the next fifteen minutes.

"Lennox, do you wanna do the honors of plugging in the star or do you want to stand back and watch?"

"I wanna watch."

I lift him from my shoulders and set him on his feet.

"Sami, can you turn the lights off? That way we can see it lit up in all its glory."

Sami flips the few switches by the door and then returns to stand by Lennox.

"Are ya ready?" I ask as I reach up to attach the star to the string of lights.

"Yep."

"Oh yeah."

Sami and Lennox reply with excitement at the same time.

I attach the cords and even though the lights wrapped around the tree are already lit, the addition of the star at the top makes it a million times better, more festive. It makes it… complete.

I glance at Sami, whose eyes are wide, and her hands are covering her mouth. Lennox has a grin that spreads across his entire face and it's full of wonder.

Damn, has he ever even had his own Christmas tree?

"What do ya think?" I ask them, pretty confident in the answer.

"It's beautiful," Sami whispers.

"It's so cool!" Lennox shouts.

"It is, isn't it?" I start to back up toward the door. "But I've got one last surprise for you in the truck. Be right back."

I whirl around and rush outside, shivering from the frigid air. As soon as I open the passenger side door, my cell phone vibrates in my back pocket. I grab it and see a notification that I have a text from Duck.

Where the fuck are you?

I glance at the time on the device and realize I should have been at the main house an hour ago. I got so caught up in making this day as fun and memorable for a certain mom and son that I totally spaced my club duties. I type out a quick reply.

Be there in 20.

I shove my phone back in my pocket and grab the small paper bag I stashed in the glove box of my truck. I run back inside, keeping it hidden behind my back, and slam the door behind me before shaking the snow out of my hair.

"Everything okay?" Sami asks, a look of concern on her face.

"Yeah," I say as I glance between her and Lennox. "I got a text from Duck. I guess I was having so much fun I forgot about our meeting this evening."

"Oh." Sami frowns. "I guess you should probably go then."

"I will but first…" I pull the bag from behind me and thrust it at them. "I wanted you both to have these."

Lennox runs up and snatches the bag from my hand. "What are they?" he asks.

"You'll just have to open it and see."

When he pulls the top of the bag apart and peers inside, his eyes light up. "Mom, they're more ornaments!"

He takes one out and notices it's not his and he runs it to his mom. Sami holds onto the red ribbon the wooden angel ornament dangles from and notices her name carved into it. She stares at it a moment before lifting her eyes to mine.

"Thank you."

"You're very welcome," I say. "Why don't you put it on the tree?"

"Mom, mom," Lennox calls. "Look at mine! It's a reindeer with my name on it."

"Awesome, baby." She gushes over his. "Wanna hang it on the tree?"

"Yeah."

Both of them hang their ornaments near the middle, right in the front. It's not lost on me that they hang them on branches right next to each other. Whether or not they realize it, they're close, even if Lennox acts like he hates her sometimes.

Sami turns back around and locks eyes with me. "When did you do this? We were together all day."

"You and Laney took the boys to get hot chocolate at the tree farm. The guy that owns the place also does these ornaments on the side. I called ahead and he had them ready so all I had to do was pick them up while we were there."

"Well, thank you. It was very thoughtful," she says and then her eyes widen. "What about you? Did you get yourself one? It's your tree. You need an ornament on it."

"Angel, I have ornaments tucked away somewhere. I'll find them and get them out." I shrug. "Besides, I wanted this to be special for you two, not me."

Sami's expression turns sad. "I guess when we leave, you'll—"

"*If* you leave, they go with you."

With Lennox right there, Sami doesn't argue. "Thanks."

"You're welcome."

"I'm hungry," Lennox says, seemingly over the whole special day thing, and I chuckle.

"I hate to do this but you two are on your own for dinner. I've gotta run to the main house for an hour or so. I'm sure you could go join Laney and Shiloh if you wanted. And I'll be back as soon as I can."

"No, no," Sami says. "I don't want to impose on them again. I'll find us something here... if you're sure that's okay?"

"Of course. Make yourselves at home." I walk back to the door and pull it open. "I'll be back soon."

SAMI

I look at the clock on the wall for what seems like the hundredth time since Snow left. He left around six and said he'd be gone for an hour or so… it's now almost one in the morning. What could he possibly be doing that's taking so long?

Visiting a girlfriend he failed to mention.

No. No, no, no. He told me he wasn't attached, and I believed him.

But how well do you really know the man? Can you trust him?

Yes. Unequivocally, yes. He's done everything he said he would and more. I mean, what grown ass man, the president of a one percenter motorcycle club no less, would take in a single mother of a boy who is less than respectful and also the son of one of his drug runners?

"Mommy?" Lennox stirs on the couch next to me, sitting up and rubbing the sleep from his eyes. "Is he home yet?"

I hug him to me. "Not yet, baby."

"Maybe we should go check on him," he suggests. "It's really cold out there and what if he fell like you did and no one knows?"

My head falls to rest on the back of the couch, and I silently thank whoever, or whatever, is up there that gave my son some of my qualities. Corey may have strong genes but so do I... and mine are better.

"Ya know what?" I say to Lennox. "Maybe we should go make sure he's okay."

Lennox doesn't need to know that I don't believe for a second that Snow *isn't* okay, but if checking on him will make my son feel better, I can do that. I *need* to do that because he deserves to know that things aren't falling apart around him.

"Go get your shoes and jacket, okay?"

Lennox scrambles off the couch and runs to the room we're sharing. I turn off the TV and fold the blanket to drape over the back of the sectional. I already cleaned up our dishes from dinner and the dishwasher is still running. I turn in a circle to make sure I'm not forgetting something. I don't want to leave his house messy.

"Ready," Lennox says as he comes skidding to a stop in front of me, boots in his hands.

"Um, those boots aren't gonna do ya any good in your hands, baby."

He rolls his eyes dramatically. "Duh."

He drops to his butt and starts putting them on. While he does that, I grab the jacket and boots out of the coat closet that Snow said I could borrow until I get my own. By the time we're both bundled up, a quick glance at the clock tells me it's quarter after one.

"Let's go," I say, grabbing a hold of Lennox's hand and leading him outside.

The compound is dark. There are motion lights surrounding the outer edge, according to Snow, so the fact that they aren't lit up gives me some peace of mind. I glance toward Laney's house and notice the porch light is on, as well as a light on the second floor. I can see shadows in the window and all I can think is 'good for her'.

The main house is right across the roadway, so we can see it from the porch, and it's lit up almost as bright as our Christmas tree.

Our?

Because the buildings are so close, I can see a man standing at the entrance Snow took us through when we first arrived, and I recognize him as Mikey, the member who beat the shit out of Corey. I look down at Lennox to see if he notices and it doesn't appear he does. Thank goodness for small favors.

"You can't go in there," Mikey says as we get close. His tone is firm, matter of fact.

"I don't know if you remem—"

"I remember who you are, Sami." He stoops down to look Lennox in the eyes and his voice softens. "And you, Lennox. I remember you. You're pretty damn strong for a little kid."

"I'm not little," Lennox counters. "And I don't remember you."

Mikey straightens and shrugs. "That's okay. Probably better that you don't."

The wind blows and I shiver. "P-please just let us in. It's cold out here."

"I can't do that."

"Of course you can," I argue and point to the keypad by the door behind him. "You just punch a code into that handy dandy thing right there and poof, the door opens."

Mikey smirks but it isn't friendly. "Oh, is that all?" He reaches toward me and suggestively rubs his hand up and down my arm. "But if you're cold..."

"Don't touch her!" Lennox shouts and hauls back his arm.

Before his fist can connect with Mikey's balls, the door

flies open, knocking Mikey forward and almost knocking me onto my ass.

Snow barrels through the opening and wraps his hand around Mikey's throat. He throws him against the wall.

"What the fuck do you think you're doing?" he snarls. "You don't ever put your hands on a woman who doesn't invite it… especially not *my* woman!"

His woman?

"Pres… I didn't mean—"

"Don't." Snow's grip tightens and Mikey's eyes widen. "Don't pretend you weren't angling for the right to warm her up."

"Snow, let him go." I settle my hand on his outstretched arm. "It's okay. I'm okay."

Snow spares me a glance and shoves himself away from Mikey. He looks over his shoulder at Lennox, who's standing there like a spectator at a UFC fight, taking it all in.

"Get your shit packed and get the fuck off the property," Snow demands of Mikey.

"Snow, that's a bit extreme, don't ya think?"

I look toward the open door and see Duck standing there, a concerned look on his face.

"Not in the fucking least," Snow snarls.

Duck looks at me. "Hey, mama, why don't you and Lennox go back to Snow's place, and he'll be there soon?"

"I'm not leaving," I say, standing my ground. I didn't do that enough with Corey—shit, I didn't do it at all—and even in this state, Snow doesn't scare me.

"Me either," Lennox says with force, folding his arms over his chest like he's six feet of solid muscle and could take on Bigfoot if he were here. "If Mom stays, I do too."

"Okay, fine." Duck heaves a sigh. "Snow, take them inside at least. They're freezing. I'll handle Mikey."

I wait for Snow to argue but he surprises me. His shoulders relax slightly, and he turns to face us. "C'mon, let's get you warmed up."

He wraps his arm around my shoulder and guides me inside, Lennox on our heels.

"This isn't over," he snarls at Mikey as he shoves past him.

Before the door closes behind us, I hear Duck's shouting at Mikey.

"What the fuck were you thinking? You know there are cameras ever…"

The steel door clicks shut and I miss the rest. I want to push it back open, hear more about these cameras, but I'm too cold to care all that much. At least right this moment.

"Angel, what are you doing here?" Snow asks as he leads Lennox and I to the couch and gently pushes me down to sit.

"We was worried," Lennox answers before I can. "You were gone a long time and we thought you might have gotten cold like Mommy and fell down and no one would find you because it's so late and I told her we should com—"

Snow chuckles as he holds his hand up to stop Lennox's rant. "Okay, I get it. You were worried." He returns his gaze to me. "But I told you I'd be home."

All the worry, all the nervousness and frustration at how long he was gone returns like a fireball and explodes out of my mouth.

"You told me you'd be home in an hour or so!" I yell, shooting to my feet. "I waited seven. Seven damn hours! Do you have any idea what it's like to be in a strange place, with people you don't know surrounding you, with worst case scenarios running through your head? Huh? Do you?"

I don't realize until I'm done yelling that we're now surrounded by other Satan's Legacy members, all sporting the same cut as Snow but with slightly different patches. My chest heaves as I try to pull air into my lungs in an effort to calm myself, but it seems impossible.

"Angel, calm—"

"Stop calling me that!" I flatten my hands on Snow's chest and shove. When he barely budges, my anger ratchets up a notch. "I'm not your angel. I'm not anyone's angel. I'm just Sami!"

Snow bobs his head as if he's agreeing with me, but his eyes say otherwise. "Okay... Sami." He glances over his shoulder at his brothers. "I think we're done for the night. Head home and we'll talk more in the morning. Be back here at ten."

When no one moves, Snow scowls. "Get. Out. Now!"

It takes a few seconds, but everyone listens. As he walks by, Magic slaps Snow on the back.

"Go easy on her, Pres," he says. "Can't be easy for her with everything going on."

Understatement of the year.

When Lennox, Snow, and I are alone, I flop back down on the couch. Lennox scoots close to me and rests his head on my shoulder. Despite all the chaos around him, it's the middle of the night and he has to be tired.

"Sami, listen," Snow begins as he sits on the other side of me. "I'm sorry if I worried you." He leans around to look at Lennox. "Both of you. I know it's not an excuse, but I'm not used to having to think about how my schedule or lifestyle affect others." He shrugs as if that explanation makes it all better. "And I'm sorry that you're caught up in something that I can't even talk about. But I promise you, you're safe here."

"Didn't feel too safe with Mikey," I mumble.

Snow's face hardens. "He'll be dealt with."

I lift my head to look Snow in the eyes. "How?"

He strokes his beard. "For starters, his patch will be stripped."

"For starters?"

Snow arches a brow. "Do you really want to know the rest?"

I think about that for a minute. Scenes from television shows pop into my head and a chill races up my spine.

"No, I don't."

"I know I've said it before, but I'll say it again. There are always going to be things I can't tell you. It's forbidden but it's also for your own safety and the safety of the club and our families. But if it's something I can share, I will."

I lean forward, pressing my fingers into my temples to stop the raging headache forming. "This is just so much, ya know? I went from one volatile situation to what feels like another. I hear what you're saying, and you've done nothing to make me think you're lying, but it's still…"

"Still what?"

I shrug, unsure of how to best explain it. I settle on simple and noncommittal.

"A lot."

"I know." Snow stands and reaches a hand out to me. "Let's go home and we can talk some more." He tips his head toward Lennox. "I think someone could use a bed to stretch out in."

I glance at Lennox, who is now sound asleep. Rather than taking Snow's hand, I twist so I can lift Lennox, but Snow stops me.

"I'll carry him."

I nod. "Thanks."

Snow, carrying Lennox, and I walk silently, side by side, across the street. There's no sign of Mikey or Duck but I'm too drained to give it much thought. When we step inside Snow's house, the Christmas tree lights greet us, and I immediately go to the couch while Snow takes Lennox to his room.

I kick off my boots and toss my jacket over the arm of the

sectional. I rest my head on the pillow that's there and stretch my legs out, getting comfy. Whatever Snow wants to talk about, it's probably nothing good, so I might as well be comfortable while being… well, uncomfortable.

"He's out like a light."

I lift my head slightly and watch Snow walking toward me. He slips off his cut and drapes it over the back of the couch.

"I'm going to go change real quick," he says as he pulls his shirt off. "Be right back."

I watch him walk toward his room, the muscles in his back bunching as he puts one foot in front of the other. As upset and mentally exhausted as I am, my body doesn't seem to get the memo, and my insides turn to molten lava at the pure sexual sin he oozes.

I can hear his boots thud on his floor, as well as his jeans and belt, and the sounds echo in my head like an unwelcome siren's song. When Snow emerges from his room in nothing but sweats, saliva pools under my tongue. No man has the right to look that damn good while a woman is still mad at them.

Are you mad? Or just really confused?

"Can I get you anything to drink?" he asks as he walks to the kitchen, bypassing the sectional completely.

I can't seem to take my eyes off his ass and when I don't answer, he looks over his shoulder. "Sami?"

I raise my head quickly and see amusement flicker in his eyes.

"Huh?"

"Do you want anything to drink?"

Yeah, you.

"Hot chocolate?"

"I think I can make that happen," he says and moves around in the kitchen getting the needed ingredients. He also pulls out a bottle of whiskey and holds it up for me to see. "Want the adult version?"

Adult version? Yes, please.

I nod vigorously.

It doesn't take him long to fix our drinks and when he walks toward me, both mugs in his hands, my eyes zero in on the way his sweats are settled low on his hips and how they hug his package.

"Here ya go."

He hands me a mug and I quickly take a sip, ignoring the fact that it burns my throat. No sense in letting him know I was so focused on his body and forgot the drink he made would be hot. The drink, and his body, should come with a big neon flashing warning label: Too hot to handle.

"Wow," he comments, blowing on his own hot chocolate to cool it before taking a sip. "Your mouth and throat must be able to handle a lot of heat."

The sexual innuendo is there, but the problem is, I can't tell if he means it sexually or if my brain is just so muddled that it's as far into the gutter as it can get.

"Yep, I can handle a lot." *Sweet baby Jesus, did I just say that?* "I mean... that's not what I—"

"It's okay, Angel," he says with a chuckle. I glare at him, but he simply shrugs. "Sorry, but it's habit and gonna be hard to break. Might as well get used to it... *Angel.*"

I try to remember why we're sitting here in the first place and finally, the reason clicks into place.

"You said we needed to talk," I remind him.

"I did," he confirms.

"So talk."

Snow sets his mug on the coffee table and twists on the couch to fully face me.

"First, I'm sorry I worried you both tonight." He holds his hand up when I open my mouth to protest. "I know I already said that, but I'm not sure you believed me. I am sorry, Sami. It's just…" He averts his gaze and stares at the blank TV screen.

"Just what?" I prod.

"You're not the only one with a shitty ex," he admits, finally returning his gaze to mine. "Marlene… that was her name."

I don't know what I was expecting from this talk but info about his past love life certainly wasn't it.

"Why was she shitty?"

Snow takes a deep breath and holds it for a minute before exhaling through his nose. "Let's just say, she brought nothing but trouble to me, my family, and this club. After her, my guard was up, and I wanted nothing more to do with women beyond what they could provide me in bed."

"Nice," I mumble.

"I've told you, I'm not a good man and I'm certainly not a saint."

I wave my hand like I couldn't care less about how many women he's slept with.

But you do care. For some insane reason, it bothers you.

"Anyway, she always asked too many questions, demanded info she knew I couldn't give. And then there's her brother." Snow's face hardens, and his hands ball into fists in his lap. "After what they did, it was hard for me to trust again. And then Lennox banged on the shelter door one night and I saw him, and you, and it was like the walls I put up started melting." He shrugs. "I can't explain it. I have no clue why, but something about the two of you latched onto my soul and wouldn't let go. And that scares the shit out of me because I'm afraid you could make me talk about things I know I can't, that you hold the power to make me cross lines I've crossed before only to get drop-kicked back across."

There's something in his tone, in his expression that

makes me believe him, believe every word he's saying. I may not like the rules and policies of the club, but I can't fault Snow for them. Sure, he's the president, and I assume he could change them, but if they're long-standing traditions, why would he? Why *should* he? Especially for a woman and child he barely knows.

"And me asking questions triggered whatever Marlene did, how you felt back then?"

"Sure did," he agrees. "But more than that, when I saw Mikey touch you, I fucking lost it."

"How did you see that, by the way?"

"Oh." He shakes his head. "We've got cameras everywhere and in the meeting room, there's a screen that allows us to see what's happening at the main entrance. For safety reasons."

"Ah, okay." I take a sip of my hot chocolate, which is much cooler by now, and savor the added whiskey. "Makes sense. But you know I can handle myself, right? I've been doing it for years."

"Don't you get it?" he snaps but without anger. "You shouldn't have to."

"Yeah, I should," I counter. "I'm a mother. If I can't take care of myself, how am I supposed to take care of my son?"

"All I'm saying is it doesn't hurt to have backup," he says and leans forward. He cups my cheek. "Or someone at your side, helping you, having your back no matter what."

Snow rubs his thumb under my eye and my lids slide closed. God, it feels so good when he touches me, and I lean into it. There was a time I'd think the same thing about Corey but that was years ago, before Lennox was born.

"Do you have any idea the things I want to do to you?" he whispers and he's so close his breath skates across my lips.

"Mmm."

Warm lips press against mine. My initial reaction is to

111

pull back. Maybe it's the alcohol, or maybe it's just me wanting him just as much, but I don't pull away. Snow's hand wraps around the back of my neck and he holds me in place, massaging with his fingers while his tongue presses the seam of my lips.

The kiss heats up and Snow grasps my hips with his free hand and tugs me so I'm laid out on the couch and he's on top of me. My legs instinctively go around him and my hands flatten on his bare chest. His heart is thumping wildly, and it seems to match my own.

"I need you," he growls into my mouth.

"I…"

Holy shit! What am I doing?

I push against him, and he immediately sits up, confusion in his eyes.

"What's wrong? What happened?"

I try to sit up but until he moves so he's not on top of me, I can't. He stands and I scoot back into a sitting position, pulling my knees to my chest.

"I can't do this," I say.

"Can't do what? Kiss me?"

I glance at him, expecting to see disgust, annoyance, anger, but all I see is concern. And not for himself, but for me.

"Did I do something wrong?" he asks, genuinely confused.

"No." I shove my fingers through my hair. "God, no. You're doing everything right."

"I fail to see the problem."

"I'm not used to that," I snap and stand to pace the room. "My entire life, the only person I could trust was myself. No one had my back. My parents tried but…" I shake my head. "They were too selfish, too codependent, too high to deal with a kid. Let alone a pregnant sixteen-year-old. They begged me to have an abortion, but I wanted no part of that. So I packed my bags and left with Corey."

"Let me guess, he promised you the world?"

I nod. "And at first, things were good," I admit. "He wasn't always like he is now. He put me first when that was not what I was used to. He made me feel loved and cherished. And then the medical bills started to come. I guess he thought having a baby was going to be free. I don't know. I ended up getting my job at the diner to help pay the bills and Corey did... he did what he had to I guess to help."

"He didn't have to run drugs, Sami. He could have gotten any other job and you all would have been just fine."

"I wish I believed that." I implore him with a look to understand. "I wish with everything in me that Lennox had a mom and dad who loved him, who loved each other. I wish Corey gave a damn about either one of us but at the end of the day, all he cares about is his next fix and how much I earn in tips so he can get it."

Snow brushes a strand of hair out of my face. "That's not love, Angel. That's abuse."

"I know that. I'm not stupid," I snap. I swipe at the falling tears I hadn't realized were there until just now. "But Lennox deserves so much better than what he's got."

"Bullshit!" Snow barks. "From what I can see, he has an amazing mother who, despite the pain it caused her, she always put her son first. He has a mom who stayed because she wanted her son to have two parents." He smiles. "I look at you and I see so much that you don't. But fuck, I wish you did. I wish you saw you the way I do, the way most people probably do."

I sniffle. "I just wish he had a family... beyond just me. What happens when I'm not here anymore? Someday, I'll be gone, and then what?"

"Ah, Angel," Snow says softly. "Lennox has a family. A

pretty fucking big one now. And one that will have his back, no matter what. The only thing you need to decide is if it's temporary or not. Because whether it makes sense and no matter how scary it is, I'm not going anywhere. Satan's Legacy isn't going anywhere. You're one of us now, which makes him one of our own, blood or not."

SNOW

ONE WEEK LATER...

"*I* really don't need an escort."

I open the door to the diner and follow Sami inside. We've talked about this for the last week, her fighting it every step of the way. If she insists on keeping her job, there will be someone there, at all times, to make sure she's okay.

"So you keep saying." I wave to one of the other waitresses who sometimes takes care of our group when we come in. "But we agreed you'd suck it up."

Sami practically growls at me but doesn't argue. She walks behind the counter and puts her bag under it, grabbing an apron as she does. I head to a booth toward the back, waiting on a few of the brothers to get here. We all agreed we'd be less conspicuous if there were more than one of us present.

"What can I get ya, Snow?" Sandy, an older waitress asks.

"My usual," I respond with a smile. "Magic, Duck, and Toga will be joining me so you might as well get their usual as well."

"No problem." She writes down the order. "I gotta say, it's nice to see you. Been a while."

"It has, Sandy, and it's good to see you too." I rest my forearms on the table. "How are the grandkids?"

"Oh you know, excited about the carnival next week. Driving their mama and me insane."

"I bet."

"Well, let me get this order in, and I'll bring out the coffee."

"Thanks, Sandy."

She winks. "Sure thing, hon."

As she walks away, I turn my attention to Sami, who's waiting on a male customer I recognize. Definitely not a man who poses a threat.

The front door opens and in walks my brothers. Each of them say hello to Sami as they pass and make their way to my booth.

"This snow needs to fucking disappear," Toga complains when he slides into the booth across from me. "I need to ride and not in a goddamn cage."

"Saw on the weather report this morning that the snow should melt in a day or two," Duck informs us all as he sits. "I'm with ya man, a ride sounds like heaven right about now."

"Boys and their toys," Sandy says when she returns with the coffee.

Magic clutches his chest dramatically. "Sandy, you're killing me. Harleys aren't toys. They're a way of life. And we are definitely not boys."

"Keep telling yourself that," Sandy teases him.

This banter is normal and if it were anyone else, we'd probably take offense. But Sandy's late husband was a biker, so we know her teasing comes from a place of love.

"Snow ordered everyone's usual," Sandy tells the guys. "Any changes to that?"

"Nope."

"Nah."

"Not a chance."

All three of them speak at once and Sandy cackles. "Didn't think so but wanted to be sure. The last thing I need is a Satan's Legacy member on my ass because they were served sausage instead of bacon."

Sandy turns to walk away, and I call her back, a thought occurring to me.

"Hey, Sandy, I have a question." She turns to face me. "Does Sami typically eat breakfast here when she has the early shift?"

Sandy tilts her head to think about it. "Not that I recall. But I'm not always here when she is so..." she shrugs. "Why?"

"No reason."

"Right," Sandy taunts. "No reason other than you've got your sights set on her and you actually found someone who you give a shit about."

"Damn, bro," Duck jokes. "She's got your number."

"Thanks, Sandy," I say, my tone clear that the conversation is over. "We'll wait for our food."

"Dude," Toga says. "What do you care what Sami eats for breakfast or where she eats it?"

"You can't be that fucking stupid," Magic accuses.

"What?" Toga asks, apparently clueless.

"Here, let me see if this tells you anything," Magic says to him and then turns to face me. "Snow, have you fucked anyone since you met Sami? Or even thought about fucking anyone since then?"

I press my lips together, knowing my answer is only going to fuel their teasing, and I'll never hear the end of it.

"Oh, shit," Toga says. "Now I get it. You fucking love her, don't you?"

"Ding, ding, ding," Duck says with his finger touching his nose. "We have a winner."

"Would you guys keep your voices down?" I whisper harshly. "It's not like this place is so big she can't hear you."

Duck leans forward. "I can't help but notice you're not denying it."

"You guys are ridiculous," I snap. "How the hell am I even supposed to answer that question? Did it even occur to you that I haven't thought about fucking anyone else because I've been busy?"

"Busy banging the single mom," Toga says.

I lunge out of my seat and across the table, knocking over both our coffees and grip his cut. "Don't you ever talk about her like that again, ya got me?"

Toga grabs my wrists and flings me off him. "Seriously, dude. You need to fucking chill. I was just joking."

"And Sami isn't a joke... not to me."

I sit back down and start wiping up the spilled drinks, pulling napkins out of the dispenser at the edge of the table as I need them. Sami rushes over with a wet rag and starts to help, her expression full of anger.

"If you guys can't behave, you can get the fuck out," she admonishes, her voice barely above a whisper. "I'm trying to work here."

"Sorry, Angel," I say. "It won't happen again." I glare at Toga. "Will it?"

He grins at Sami. "No, ma'am, it sure won't."

"It better not."

She walks away from the table after our mess is cleaned up and I can't help but stare at the sway of her hips.

"Yep, a total goner," Duck observes.

"Shut up," I snap.

But I don't argue with them anymore because they're right. I am a goner. I was a goner the moment I laid eyes on her. I went further down the hole when I picked them up at that McDonald's and then there was the day of Christmas fun. Add in the last week and I'm fucked.

I love her and I have no goddamn clue what to do about it because I don't believe for a second those feelings are reciprocated.

"Thanks, Sandy," I say as she clears our plates. "Food was great, as always."

"Uh huh." She glances over her shoulder at Sami. "I'm guessing the view had more to do with that than the flavor profiles."

When she's out of ear shot, I lean forward. "Okay, time to get down to business."

"You really want to talk shop here, in public?" Duck asks.

"Gotta do it sometime and I'm not leaving here today so yeah, I do."

"Okay." He shrugs.

"From what I gather, things with Corey are heating up. The run last week went as planned and Magic," I turn to him. "You said you felt like he didn't suspect a thing, right?"

"Right," he confirms. "We told him we were switching suppliers so his next drop might not be for a while. He wasn't happy about it, but we gave him a little personal stash to tide him over and that seemed to calm him down. Dude's a fucking tweaker, not a good dealer."

"But from what's been reported, he's started asking a lot of questions."

"That's true," Toga confirms. "He's texted me at least a dozen times saying he's got customer's hounding him for product. I don't know if that's actually what's happening or if he's snorted and shot his way through what we gave him."

"What have you told him?"

"Exactly what you instructed," Toga states. "We're still working out the details with the new supplier and we'll get him what we can as soon as we have it."

"Asshole isn't accepting that info though," Magic cuts in. "He's texting all of us, twisting our words and trying to play us all against each other."

"Okay, I'm thinking we need to move on the timeline." I stroke my beard. "I wanted to wait until after the carnival but I don't know if we can afford to do that. It's too risky to have him out there while that's going on."

"Pres, I hear ya," Duck says. "But I don't think we have time to move things up. There's still a lot to do and we have less than a week until the carnival. I think our best bet is to call on some other chapters for help with security at the carnival. It's a festival thrown by bikers so having more there isn't going to even register to people."

I lean back and think over our options. On one hand, Corey needs to go. I'm tired of always waiting for what the punk is gonna do next. He was never someone I worried about and then Sami and Lennox came along, and I can't get him out of my head. On the other hand, Duck's right: pulling off the Christmas carnival and taking out Corey would be a lot to get done in such a short time.

"Fine," I reluctantly agree. "Duck, call Grizzly in Portland and see if he can spare anyone to help. Call any other chapters within a few hundred miles. We've got the house on the compound that can sleep up to twelve and then whatever beds are left in the prospect house. I'm sure the rest of us can spare a room if we get enough of them willing to come and help."

"I'll get on it as soon as I leave here," Duck agrees.

"Good." I heave a sigh. "Next thing we need to discuss is Mikey."

"I handled that," Duck says.

"Did you?" I counter. "Because I'm pretty sure I saw him in the main house yesterday, still wearing a cut and patch like he belonged there."

"Stripping a member of his patch has to be put to a vote," Magic says. "I know why you're pissed at him, Snow, and I agree he's gotta go. He crossed a line. But we've gotta do it right."

"No, we just need him gone," I bark. "He crossed a fucking line, and he knew exactly what he was doing."

"Agreed," Toga says. "But we have bylaws and policies for a reason. We break them now, for this, what's next?"

A growl barrels out of my throat. "Fine. We meet on this tonight. I don't care if anyone has any other plans, tell 'em to cancel them."

"I'll send out a mass text," Duck says.

I breathe a sigh of relief. I expected more of an argument. I know I overreacted to what Mikey did. It was a simple touch, but if I let that slide, then what? A touch can lead to so much more and regardless of what we do, Satan's Legacy members will never do anything that makes a woman feel unsafe. Cross that line and you might as well buy a one-way ticket to Hell.

"Why don't you guys go do what you need to do today?" I say, knowing there's a lot that needs to be handled. "Oh, and Duck, pay the bill on your way out." I grin.

"Of course, but you'll owe me."

SAMI

I watch Duck, Magic, and Toga disappear out of the diner and make my way to sit at the table with Snow.

"Hey, Angel," he says with a smile. "Break time?"

"I've got a few minutes."

"Why don't you have something to eat? I don't think I've seen you stop moving since you walked in."

"I'm fine. I'll get a lunch break in a few hours, and I'll eat then."

He pushes his glass of water that Sandy has kept filled toward me. "Here, at least hydrate."

I wrap her fingers around the glass and lift it to my lips, drinking it until it's almost gone.

I wipe my mouth with the back of my hand. "Thanks. I guess I was thirsty." I move to scoot out of the booth. "I'll go get you a refill."

Snow grabs my hand when I get to my feet and pulls me to sit next to him. "Sandy'll get the refill. You're on a break, remember?"

Before I can argue, the door to the diner crashes open and

heads turn to see who entered. Snow narrows his eyes and his muscles tense when he sees who it is.

Corey swivels his head until his eyes land on who he seems to be searching for: me.

I stiffen and when I start to move away from Snow, he wraps his arm around my shoulders and holds me in place.

"Don't, Angel," he whispers. "Let me handle this, okay?"

I give a slight nod, but my eyes widen as Corey stalks toward us, rage in his expression and purpose in his stride.

"You fucking bitch," he seethes when he reaches our table. "Where's my son?"

"Why don't you have a seat, Corey?" Snow offers, nodding at the other side of the booth. "We'll be more than happy to talk to you if you sit and calm the fuck down."

Almost as if he had tunnel vision when he saw me, hearing Snow's voice seems to snap Corey out of whatever snit he's in.

"Oh, hey, man," Corey says casually. "Been a while."

"I know exactly how long it's been," Snow snarls. "Now, I suggest you sit down, and we can all talk like adults, or you and I can take whatever this is outside. Regardless, Sami isn't talking to you alone so…"

Corey smiles like him showing up here is for a normal chat. He slides into the booth and looks at me. "Get me a glass of water, honey."

"She's on a break," Snow says. "And even if she weren't, she wouldn't be getting you shit."

"It's okay," I say and try to pull away from Snow.

"No, it's not okay," he snarls, never taking his eyes off Corey. "You don't owe him anything, Angel."

Corey throws his head back and laughs. "Oh my God, she has you snowed… no pun intended, bro." He shakes his head. "But she's the furthest thing from an angel as someone can get."

Snow removes his arm from around me and slams a fist onto the tabletop. "First off, you will not speak about her like that. I don't give a shit if she cut your dick off and fed it to you. She's the mother of your son and you'll treat her with respect." Snow takes a deep breath and deepens his scowl. "Second, I'm not your bro. Never have been and never will be. I'm your employer and even that will be up for debate if you keep your shit up."

"Whatever, man," Corey grumbles and shifts his attention to me. "I came here to see you anyway."

"What do you want, Corey?" I ask, almost afraid of the answer.

"I thought that was pretty clear," he responds. "I want to see my son."

"That's not gonna happen," Snow snarls.

Corey glares at him. "I wasn't talking to you."

I tilt my head. "Why do you want to see Lennox? You kicked us out, remember?"

"Do I need a reason?" Corey counters.

"Actually, yeah," I say. "You do. Because I'm tired of you treating us like we're trash. And I won't stand for it anymore. Lennox deserves better. *I* deserve better."

"Sami, baby," Corey begins and tips his head at Snow. "He's gonna get you and *our* son killed. Do you have any idea what he and his club are into?"

The word 'baby' makes me cringe, but the rest of his statement has my insides twisting. I have an idea what they do but I'm sure there's plenty I can't even imagine.

"Didn't think so," Corey says when I remain quiet. He smirks. "Murder, drugs, weapons… you name it, they do it. Is that really who you want to tie yourself to, who you want influencing *our* son?"

"That's enough," Snow sneers and reaches across the table.

I rest my hand on his arm and urge him to pull it back. He does.

"No, Snow, it's okay."

I'm not sure I believe my own words, but I know that, despite what I don't know about Satan's Legacy, I can trust them more than Corey.

I think.

"Corey, you need to leave. The only time I ever want to see your face again is when we go to court because you better believe I'm going to be filing for full custody of Lennox. You will never see him again. And ya know what? It's not because of Snow or Satan's Legacy or even me. It's because of you. It's because you've done nothing but lie and put yourself first. You're not a parent. You're a fucking leach."

Corey stands up and shoves his hands in his pockets. "I hope like hell his cock is worth it, you stupid slut. Because that's going to be the reason you lose Lennox. Don't think for one second I'm above doing whatever it takes to make you suffer, even if that means taking on the brat."

With those words, he storms out of the diner. When he disappears down the sidewalk, I realize my entire body is trembling. Nausea hits me out of nowhere, and I race out of the booth, toward the bathroom. I make it in just in time to drop to my knees and vomit up the water I guzzled a few minutes earlier.

The door to the restroom creeks open and I reach up to flush the toilet.

"Hon, why don't you go home?"

Relief hits me hard when it's Sandy's voice and not Snow's.

"She's right, Angel. You should go home and rest."

And there goes the relief.

"I'm fine," I say, my voice shaky. "Can you just give me a few minutes? Please?"

"Sure thing, hon," Sandy says, and I hear the door creek again.

Thinking I'm alone, I stop trying to hold it back and dry heave until my stomach cramps. A large hand rests on my back while another pulls my hair out of my face, startling me.

"Aw, Angel," Snow croons. "Let it out."

And I do, even though it's only stomach acid. I haven't eaten since dinner the night before so after expelling the water, dry heaving is my only option.

"He's not going to take Lennox from you," Snow says. "You know that, right?"

I shake my head, unable to speak. When the dry heaving seems to stop, I fall back against Snow, letting his arms come around me. I lean my head on his arm and let the tears fall. I let myself cry because I don't know how much more I can take. I lost my family. I can't lose my son too.

Snow shifts and the next thing I know, I'm being lifted off the floor and carried out of the bathroom. I press my face into his chest so I don't have to see the nosy stares of customers.

"I'm taking her home," Snow says to someone. "She'll call to discuss her schedule moving forward."

"Take care of her." Okay, he's talking to Sandy. I can handle that. Sandy adds, "And she can take as much time off as she needs. Her job will be waiting for her when she's ready."

"Thanks, Sandy," he says.

I feel weight added when Sandy sets my jacket and purse on top of me, but Snow doesn't seem bothered by the addition. He carries me outside and straps me into the passenger side of his truck.

When he gets in on the driver's side, I don't have the energy to lift my head from the window.

"Ready to go home?" he asks.

126

Home? I don't even know where that is. When I stop and think about it, the first place that pops into my head is Snow's place. But that's supposed to be temporary.

Screw it. If it's temporary or permanent, it doesn't matter at this moment. It's where I want to be.

"Yeah, take me home."

SNOW

"*E*veryone shut the fuck up and sit down!"

I nod my thanks at Duck and take my own seat. After the events at the diner, I felt it imperative we all got together to discuss Corey. And then there's the little matter of Mikey being stripped of his patch. Mikey's present and has no clue that's going to be voted on, but he'll find out quickly enough.

"As I'm sure you've heard by now, Corey showed up at the diner this morning during Sami's shift," I say, kicking things off.

"Jesus, Pres, I hate he put her through that," Brady says. "I went in later for lunch and Sandy told me how upset Sami was."

"Leave it to Sandy to open her mouth," I grumble.

"She didn't mean any harm," Brady assures me. "I asked where Sami was because I hadn't heard she went home early. She knew she could trust me with the info."

I wave my hand. "Yeah, I know. Sandy's too damn sweet to be a gossip."

"What's the plan for Corey?" Magic asks. "We can't let him get away with this."

"Oh, we're not," I snarl. "He's as good as dead. Just have to figure out the when and how."

"I hate to be the one to throw a wrench into things but what about what Sami and Lennox want?" Toga asks. "He is Lennox's dad and regardless of the shithead he is, Lennox loves him. And Sami... I don't know. I don't get the vibe from her that she wants him dead."

"I'm not too sure about Lennox," I admit. "But Sami? We talked about it. She wants him gone... whatever that looks like. She just doesn't want to know the details."

"I know Lennox loves his dad but he's seven," Duck interjects. "Wouldn't it be better to lose him now than later? I mean, he'll have a great dad for the rest of his life."

"What the fuck is that supposed to mean?" I bark.

"Oh, c'mon," Duck says. "Let's not pretend you're not planning on stepping in and filling that role. You already have, as much as you've been able to in the last week and a half."

I hang my head. Do I want to be a dad? Fuck yes. Am I ready to be a dad? I think so. Does Lennox want me as his dad? No goddamn clue. How does Sami feel about me? No goddamn clue.

"Let's not get ahead of ourselves," I say.

"Okay, I have to say this." Duck stands and focuses his attention on me. "Zeke, I've known you your entire life. Most times I think I know you better than you know yourself." He folds his arms over his chest. "Like it or not, whether it makes sense to you or anyone else or not, you love Sami. She's it for you. You've always wanted a family, beyond what you have with Laney and Shiloh and us." He sweeps his hand to indicate the brothers in the room. "Why are you fighting it so hard?"

"Because it's been less than two weeks!" I shout, rising from my chair, frustrated that he's described exactly how I feel, and I still can't accept it. I hang my head and drop back down to sit. "And what if she doesn't feel the same?"

"Do you really think she'd be here if she didn't feel something for you?" Duck counters. "Because I've met a lot of single mothers and—"

"Fucked a lot of 'em too," Magic jokes.

"That too," Duck admits. "The point I'm trying to make is some of them were in very similar situations as Sami and do you see any of them around? No. Because they didn't need me, or they didn't want me or whatever. Feelings weren't involved with them and me. For you and Sami, there's nothing but feelings. Feelings and a whole lotta fucking passion."

"You should see the way she looks at you, Pres," Toga adds. "Like you fucking hung the moon or something. I don't know how she feels but I think you both owe it to each other to figure it the hell out."

I heave a sigh. "This is not why we're meeting. Let's get back on track," I demand. "What are we going to do about Corey?"

"I vote we put the matter on hold until you talk to Sami," Duck says.

"I second that," Magic agrees.

"Third."

"Fourth."

And so it goes until it's decided for me that I have to have a conversation I'm not sure I'm ready for, let alone I have no fucking clue how to start. How does a man ask the woman he loves if she's okay with him killing her baby daddy?

Not in those words, that's for damn sure.

"On to the next order or business," I declare. "Mikey, please stand."

Mikey's eyes narrow slightly with worry, but he does as he's told. "What's up, Pres?"

"All in favor of stripping Mikey of his patch, say 'aye'."

"What?!" Mikey shouts. "Why would my pat—"

"Aye."

"Aye."

"Aye."

And again, so it goes. Every single vote is in favor of stripping his patch.

"Let this be a lesson to all of you," I say. "You never fucking lay a hand on a woman unless she invites it. And you better be ready for your grave if you touch another brother's woman without his permission. I get that some of you are okay with sharing but I'm fucking not. Got it?"

"I think we got it, Pres," Magic says.

I walk around the table to stand behind Mikey. "Take off your cut," I demand, and he simply stands there, no doubt in shock. I bend to pull the knife out of my boot and hold it to his throat. "Take. Off. Your. Fucking. Cut."

He slips it off his shoulders and tosses it on the table.

"Duck, handle that," I instruct.

Duck grabs the cut and drops it into a metal trash can on the other side of the room. He pulls a Zippo lighter out of his pocket, the one he brings to every meeting, for just this purpose. After lighting it, he tosses it into the trash can and the cut goes up in flames.

"Next vote," I say. "Does Mikey get to live or die?"

I go around the table until all members have voted: five for live and four for die.

I press the blade to Mikey's throat until blood is drawn, but not so hard that I'm ignoring the vote.

"Mikey, I guess this is your lucky day. You've got one hour to clear out." I look at Dip and Magic. "I want you two on him until he's off the property, got it?"

"Got it," they say in unison.

I remove my knife and shove Mikey toward the door. "Get the fuck outta here before I forget that the bylaws require me to go with the majority."

It takes him a second but Mikey rushes from the room, fury in his steps. Dip and Magic are right behind him, and I trust them to ensure nothing bad happens and that he clears out.

"Anything else left to discuss tonight?" I ask.

"Nope," Duck says. "Carnival is ready to go. I spoke to the other chapters, and we'll have sixteen additional members for added security. Other than that, we'll wait to hear from you about Corey."

I nod. "Meeting adjourned."

Those remaining file out of the room but Duck stays behind.

"Need something?" I ask, brow arched.

"Zeke, seriously man, I meant what I said earlier."

"I know you did."

"So what are you gonna do about it?"

"Does it matter?" I ask.

"On so many levels, yes."

"Enlighten me."

"She's not Marlene, and Corey isn't Cedric. Don't let what they did to you, Laney, and Shiloh fuck up your chance at a future," he says. "And she's not your mother. If she feels about you the way you feel about her, she's a lifer. She won't walk. She won't take Lennox from you."

"It's not that easy to forget about all of that, ya know?" I remind him.

"I know," he conceded. "Zeke, brother, all I'm saying is don't let fear control your life. You don't do it when it comes to the club. You're scared of nothing. So why are you doing it when it comes to your heart?"

"Because they're two very different things, the club and my heart."

He stares at me for a moment and then huffs out a breath.

"Are they though?"

SAMI

"*H*e's a good guy, ya know?"

I lift my glass of wine to my lips and swallow the last bit before setting it on the peninsula in Snow's kitchen. I pour myself some more and then hold the bottle out to Laney, but she shakes her head.

"Seriously, Sami," Laney continues. "Zeke may be stubborn and a little pushy, but deep down, he's a damn teddy bear."

I think about how he's treated Lennox over the last week and a half. An image of Lennox on Snow's shoulders while decorating the tree pops into my mind and I smile.

"I know he's a good guy, Laney," I tell her. "It's just…"

"What?"

I shrug. "It's been less than two weeks. And in my experience, when something seems too good to be true, it usually is."

"With Zeke, what you see is what you get," Laney says and takes another sip of wine before refilling her glass. "He doesn't hide who he is, what the club has made him, but he counters it with so much good that all the negative doesn't seem to matter."

"So there is negative?" I ask, feeling like I caught her in a lie.

"Not like that," she insists. "Satan's Legacy is a bunch of rough and tumble guys who do whatever it takes to get the job done. But in their souls, they're good guys, honest men who treat those they love like they're gold."

"And what exactly is the job? I know about the drugs, thanks to Corey. But I don't know anything else. Snow won't tell me anything."

"The drugs are the biggest thing."

"Corey mentioned murder and weapons."

"Corey's a liar and you shouldn't believe a word that comes out of his mouth," Laney protests, almost too much.

"See, that's just it. He's a liar, yes, but in my experience, it's usually only to save his own ass. What would bringing up murder and weapons get him?"

"Have you asked Zeke about it?"

I cock my head and give her a droll look. "Like he'd tell me."

"I bet you'd be surprised at what he'd tell you."

I shake my head. "It doesn't matter. Lennox and me being here… it's temporary."

"It doesn't have to be." She grins lopsidedly at me, and I can't help but wonder if the wine she's consumed is getting to her head. "I mean, have you even tested out the goods yet?"

"I am not answering that about your brother," I say, trying not to choke on my wine as I laugh.

"All I know is, I wouldn't tie myself to anyone before knowing if there was chemistry out of *and in* the bedroom." She giggles and tries to wink but ends up blinking instead. "One thing you'll learn if you're here for any length of time is you'll hear stories, and plenty of them are ones you wouldn't want to hear to save your life. But alas, I've heard them. You should give it a go and see how you two are under all circumstances."

"Give what a go?"

I whirl around and see Snow standing right behind me, hands on his hips, smirk firmly in place.

"Laney, it's nice to see you but you can go now," he says to his sister.

Laney lifts her glass to her lips and realizes she's already drained it. She carries it to the sink to rinse it out and then calls out to her son. "Shiloh, time to go."

Shiloh and Lennox come running down the hall, sliding on the hardwood floor and running into the sectional.

"Mom," Shiloh wines. "I wanna stay." He turns to Snow. "Can't I spend the night, Uncle Zeke?"

Before Snow can even open his mouth, Laney responds. "No!"

Snow looks at her suspiciously. "Laney, I really don't—"

"No, not tonight," she insists. "Everyone has had a long day and… and besides, Shiloh, you've got a little more schoolwork to finish before Christmas break." Laney's eyes light up and she looks at me. "Actually, why doesn't Lennox spend the night at our house, and he can finish up the work with Shiloh and then they'll both be done?"

I roll my eyes at her because she's being super obvious, at least to me. I can't tell if Snow realizes what she's doing but if he doesn't, he's not as smart as I think he is.

Snow gives me a questioning look and all I can do is shrug. My brain is now tied up with all the ways Snow and I can use the house when we have it all to ourselves. The couch, the kitchen counter, the bed, shower, floor… you name it, I'm picturing it.

"Yeah, yeah," I rush to say. "I think that's a great idea."

"Yes!" Lennox says and pumps his fist in the air.

"Don't even worry about grabbing clothes," Laney says. "We've got plenty." She wraps her arms around the boy's shoulders. "Let's get going. It's getting late."

"It's not even six—"

"It's late," Laney snaps at her brother.

He holds his hands up and wisely stays silent while she herds the boys outside. I walk to the door to watch my son leave for his first sleepover and can't help the emotion that comes over me. Maybe it's the wine but something tells me it's not.

"Be good, Lennox," I call out the door. "Listen to Aunt Laney!"

The second the words are out, I slap a hand over my mouth and whirl around to face Snow. His eyes are wide but the grin he's sporting tells me he likes what he heard.

"Aunt Laney, huh?" he asks as he walks toward me.

I shake my head.

"Yeah," he says. "Pretty sure that's what you said."

I drop my hand. "It was just a figure of speech," I insist.

He threads his fingers through my hair. "Uh huh."

I shake my head, but my body is silently begging him to take me. "Really, just a figure of spee—"

My words are cut off by Snow fusing his lips to mine. All of my worries fly out the window the moment he touches me. He lifts me in his arms and presses me against the wall, his body holding me in place while his hands explore me through my clothes.

Snow shifts one hand to move under my shift and cups my breast. "Is this what Laney was talking about?" he asks, breaking the kiss and locking eyes with me. "When she said 'give it a go', was she talking about fucking me?"

My lungs seize because my pussy is screaming 'yes' but my mind isn't quite sure what answer he is looking for.

"Answer me," he growls.

"Y-yes."

Snow sets me on my feet and turns away to walk toward the kitchen.

"Wh-what are you doing?" I ask, following after him.

"Checking to see just how much alcohol you've had."

He looks in the trash and sees one empty bottle and then glances at the half empty one on the counter.

"Are you drunk?" he asks me.

"No."

"Was Laney?"

"She was… tipsy," I admit, just not realizing that her watching the boys may not have been the best thing to agree to.

Snow pulls out his cell phone and sends a text.

"What are you doing?" I ask, trying to snatch it out of his hand. "Don't get mad at her. She was just trying to help."

"I'm not doing anything to her," he says and sets his phone on the counter. "I texted Magic and told him to go to Laney's house and make sure they're okay. Told him to stay until they were all asleep."

"Oh." My shoulders slump. "So you're not mad?"

"Why would I be mad?"

"I don't know. Because we were talking about you, about…" I drop my voice to a whisper. "… sex."

Snow chuckles. "Angel, whatever is about to happen between us isn't going to be just sex."

"It isn't?"

"No." He takes a step toward me. "There are a few things we need to discuss first, but once we're done with that?" He flattens his hand between my tits and slides it down to the top of my jeans, flicking the snap open easily. "The things I'm going to do to you…" He slips his hand into my panties and presses a finger against my clit. "Let's just say, Santa's coming early."

Snow moves his finger to between my legs and curls it into my folds causing my legs to quiver. Before my knees go so weak I collapse, he removes his hand, lifts me up, and sets me on the counter.

"But first, we talk." He punctuates his statement by sucking my juices off his finger and rolling his eyes like it's the best thing he's ever tasted.

"Talk... what do we need to talk about?" I ask, talking the furthest thing from my mind.

"Us," he answers quickly. "Lennox." He pauses and takes a deep breath. "Corey."

"I told you, I don't give a shit what happens to Corey, I just don't want to know about it."

"And I heard that, loud and clear but it was brought to my attention that killing him might not be what's best for Lennox."

"What's best for Lennox is having Corey out of his life for good," I snap. "I'd rather he not have a father at all than have Corey filling his head with bullshit." I glare at him. "Next."

Snow nods. "Us."

"What about us?"

"Is there an us? Because I gotta say, to me, there is."

This question isn't as easy to answer because as crazy as it seems, I feel something for him. Love? Maybe. Lust? Definitely. Safety and security? Absolutely.

"This shouldn't be such a hard question to answer," Snow complains.

"Shouldn't it?" I counter. "You have to remember, it's not only my heart I have to think about. I have a son, one who deserves the world. I can't just jump into a relationship, especially when he's still so attached to his dad."

"I'm not asking you to jump into a relationship. I'm asking you if you have feelings for me."

"Feelings? Yes," I admit. "I do, Zeke. I like you, a lot. You've shown me in so many ways what kind of man I deserve. And you've been nothing but wonderful with Lennox. But it's not that simple."

"Why not?"

"Because you're not his dad," I cry. "Zeke, I'd give anything for that to be different, for my life to have been different, but I can't change the past."

"Do you realize you call me Zeke when you're talking about something that matters to you? At least right now you are."

The switch in topic has my head spinning and I shake it to try and keep up.

"And you're right," he says. "I'm not Lennox's dad. But since when does blood make a family? It sure as shit doesn't in my world."

I flatten my hand on my forehead. "You're saying all the right things, but…"

"But what?"

"But I've got questions, concerns."

"Okay, ask me, talk to me, Sami," he pleads.

"What did Corey mean when he said murder and weapons?" I blurt out. "Laney wouldn't tell me."

"That's because Laney doesn't know," he says.

Snow steps between my legs and rests his hands on the counter beside my hips. "I've told you, there are things that cannot be discussed with people who aren't Satan's Legacy members, and that includes relatives and spouses."

"And when it comes to me making a decision that is going to affect the life of my son, that's not okay with me."

Snow hangs his head and sighs. "You're gonna be the death of me, ya know that?"

"I'm not trying to be. I'm trying not to let you be the death of me and Lennox."

His head snaps up and his eyes lock on mine. "What I tell you right now stays right here, between us. If it gets out that I told you anything, that could mean the end of my life, and yours and Lennox's, got it?"

I nod.

He takes a deep breath. "As for the weapons, yes, we deal in weapons as well as drugs. We're very selective about our clientele though and have yet to have it bring trouble to the compound."

"And the murder?"

"We don't set out to kill, Sami." He shifts a hand to my hip and grips it. "But we do kill when we have to. And I'm not gonna lie and say I hate that part of the life, because I don't. It lets the darker side of me out to unleash its wrath on those who deserve it. And there are others of us who enjoy the hell out of it. But to just wake up one day and decide to kill someone for the hell of it? No, none of us do that. We only take the lives of people in the name of protecting those we love, protecting the club, protecting what's right." He pauses. "Although, it's very tempting to forget all our rules when it comes to Corey."

I let his explanation sink in. I try to avert my gaze, but he grips my chin and forces me to hold his stare. "Don't look away from me. I can take anything you want to sling my way, but don't look away because the thought that you can't even look me in the eyes because you hate what you see tears me apart inside."

"I didn't look away because I can't look at you," I admit. "I tried to look away because I'm terrified of the fact that everything you just told me doesn't make me want to run."

"No?"

I shake my head. "God help me, I like you. Hell, I think

I'm falling in love with you and that scares the shit out of me. There was a time I thought Corey was the answer to all my prayers, the road to all my dreams coming true. What if I'm wrong about you too?"

"You're not wrong, Angel," he says just before his lips crash into mine.

SNOW

"*Now*, Zeke. I need you now."

I lift Sami off the counter and carry her to my bedroom, kicking the door shut behind us. I set her on her feet and start stripping off my clothes.

"What are you waiting for?" I demand when she just stands there. "Get naked."

Sami continues to remain still, entirely focused on each piece of my clothing I remove from my body. When I'm fully exposed to her, cock jutting out begging for her touch, I close the distance between us.

"I'm all yours, Angel," I whisper, pressing my lips to her ear. "But I want you to be all mine."

Sami nods but again, doesn't move. I grip the bottom hem of her shirt and strip it over her head, exposing her pebbled nipples through her pink lace bra. Next, I slip my thumbs in her leggings and shove them over her hips, taking her panties with them. She's barefoot, so I bend down and pull the fabric from her body and toss it to the floor. As I stand, I lick my way up the inside of her left leg and drag my fingertips up the inside of her right leg.

ANDI RHODES

"Zeke," she moans.

I don't respond, instead standing to my full height and reaching around her to flick the clasp of her bra so it falls from her shoulders. Her full tits are on display, and I roll one between my fingers while I suck the other into my mouth, swirling her tongue around it.

"Now, Zeke."

"Not yet, Angel," I say. "Don't you dare come yet."

"You don't understand," she pleads. "It's been so long..." Her body trembles. "I don't think I can stop it."

I take a step back, removing my hands and mouth from her body. "I'll make you a deal."

"Anything," she sighs. "I'll do anything... I just need to come."

"You can come as many times as you want, but you have to give up control to me, trust me to take you higher than you've ever been."

"Deal."

I lift her in my arms, and she wraps her legs around my waist. My dick connects with her warm, wet pussy and all I want to do is plunge inside of her until we're one, but not yet. I carry her to the bed and drop her onto the mattress. She doesn't release her legs, bringing me down with her.

"Angel," I coax. "We had a deal."

Sami lets her legs fall to the sides until she's wide open for me. And I take advantage of it. I kneel on the floor and pull her so her ass is right on the edge of the bed and bury my face between her legs.

"Oh, fuck," she moans when my tongue touches her clit.

I shove a finger in her pussy while my tongue works its magic, curling the digit to intensify her pleasure. Within seconds of the combination, Sami's legs quiver uncontrollably, and her hips fly off the bed. I rest my free arm across her stomach to hold her down but otherwise, don't let up. I lap at her like a starving man and when her body begins to calm, I lift my head to see her face.

"That's one," I say.

"I can't hand—"

I crawl up her body and suck a nipple into my mouth, alternating between suckling and nipping. I shove a finger in her cunt again and her body bucks. My cock needing some contact, I release her nipple and remove my finger to flip her over to her stomach.

"Scoot toward the wall," I command.

She does and as soon as I'm confident she won't hurt her knees, I flatten on top of her, my front to her back, pressing my cock between her ass cheeks, craving the friction. I reach between her and the bed and flick her clit and lean toward her ear.

"Move your hips, Angel," I whisper. "Take what you need."

Sami starts rocking her hips, fucking the bed, her clit taking all my finger has to give. I rock my hips in rhythm with hers, letting my dick slide up and down between her perfect cheeks, trying like hell not to come.

Her body tenses as another orgasm hits her. I increase the pressure on her clit, intensifying her satisfaction as much as possible. Again, when she calms, I flip her over.

"That's two."

Her eyes drift closed but I'm not done yet. I line my dick up with her slit and push the tip in. Her eyes shoot open at the action. I still, not wanting to hurt her, knowing she said it's been a while, but she has no such problem. Sami lifts her hips, digging her heels into the mattress for support, until I'm balls deep.

"Ahhhh," I groan.

"Give me number three, Zeke," she demands.

I shift my arms and grab onto hers to raise them above her head and pin them to the mattress. She is completely at my mercy and based on the complete look of oblivion on her face, she's loving every second.

I pull out of her and slam right back in. I thrust my hips so fast, so hard, my balls slap against her skin. The entire time, I look her in the eyes and when she tries to close them, I demand she keep them open.

"Fuck me harder, Zeke," she begs. "I need more."

I increase the pace and push myself as hard as I can. Her fingers curl around mine and her nails dig into my flesh.

"More," she pleads. "Kiss me."

I smash my lips against hers, my tongue thrusting in time with my hips. She's already come twice, and I'm not sure I can last long enough to get her to a third time.

"Gotta help me, Angel," I say from between clenched teeth. "Help me get you to three."

Sami shoves her hand between us and rubs her clit. That, coupled with our animalistic fucking pushes her over the edge. Her pussy clenches and my balls tingle.

"That's it," I growl.

"Come with me Zeke," she commands.

Those four words are all it takes to push me over the ledge. I lose myself inside her as she milks me for all I've got. Neither of us slow down, although she does remove her hand and grab my ass cheek to hold me close. My body jerks as her hips buck, both of us riding out the fall.

When my muscles unclench, I collapse, rolling to the side as I do so I don't crush her. I pull her with me, and she tucks her head into my shoulder.

"That's one," she says sleepily.

I kiss her forehead. "Ah, Angel, it's three. And those are the only three that matter."

Sami lifts her head and shakes it. "No. Your pleasure is just important."

I grin. "You don't get it, do you?"

"Get what?"

"Making you happy, bringing you pleasure... It brings me both too because I love you."

SAMI

"We're gonna be late, Mom."

I stare at Snow's reflection in the mirror and can't help but laugh at his grin. His arms are wrapped around me, and it feels right… perfect. The entire last week has felt like that.

"Yeah, Mrs. Claus, we're gonna be late," Snow says.

I shake my head at him. Lately, it feels like he and Lennox are ganging up on me, but not in a bad way. And honestly, it's refreshing to see Lennox acting like a normal seven-year-old and not like Corey.

I turn in Snow's arms and tug on his beard. "Okay, Santa, let's get moving. Wouldn't want to disappoint the kids, now would we?"

How I got roped into being Mrs. Claus for the carnival, I have no idea. Although I suspect it has something to do with a girl's night with Laney, and her plying me with alcohol and begging me to do it so she wouldn't have to pretend to be her brother's wife.

"No, we sure wouldn't."

Snow and I walk into the living room and Lennox takes one look at us and doubles over laughing.

"What's so funny?" Snow says, advancing on Lennox.

Lennox takes off running around the sectional, Snow chasing after him.

"Nothing," Lennox cries out with laughter. "Nothing is funny."

Snow catches him and tosses him into the air. Tears burn the back of my eyes at the sight because it's so normal. And Lennox is loving it. Hearing my little boy laugh, seeing him happy... It's everything to me.

And having Snow be the one to make it happen doesn't hurt either. Because I love the man.

"Put me down," Lennox says, still laughing. "We gotta go."

Snow puts Lennox down and straightens to look at me. "The little elf is right, Mrs. Claus. We have to go."

"I'm not an elf," Lennox protests.

"Those ears say otherwise, baby," I tell him, pointing to the part of his costume he hated the most when we showed him.

My son rolls his eyes, but he smiles. "Fine. I'm an elf. But only for tonight, okay?"

"You got it," Snow agrees.

We all walk to the door and put our jackets on but Snow grabs two boxes out of the closet and hands them to us before we leave.

"What're these?" I ask, grabbing one while Lennox takes the other.

"Helmets," he responds matter-of-factly.

"For what?"

"The snow has finally cleared up and I figure we should show up in style."

"I'm not getting on your bike," I say, panic flaring.

"Yes, you are," he says. "And you'll be fine. I even added a side care for our little elf." He grins. "Which, by the way, never happens, so smile and say thank you and let's be on our way."

"Zeke, we're not getting on that thing," I argue.

"Dude, she used your real name," Lennox says. "That's never good."

Ignoring Lennox's jibe, Snow lifts my hands. "Sami, do you trust me?"

"Of course." My response is immediate.

"Then trust me when I say, we'll be perfectly safe on my bike. I'll even take it slow, just for you."

"But I wanna go fast," Lennox whines.

"No," I say. "We're not going fast."

"But we're going, right?" my son asks. "Because you said we're not going fast so that means we're going and we're going slow."

Damn my son and his logic.

"Fine," I cave. "Slow, though."

And that's exactly what Snow does. He takes us to the Christmas carnival, nice and slow, as promised. We arrive in one piece, and even though I won't admit it any time soon, I can't wait to get on the back of that Harley, without the sidecar and my son, and go fast… really fast.

When we arrive, the carnival is in full swing. There are bikers everywhere and people who would normally cross the street to avoid them are interacting and having a great time. There are rides, food trucks, vendors, games, a bounce house, and so much more.

"How did you manage to pull this off?" I ask Snow.

"With a lot of help," he chuckles. "We've got some great volunteers and all of the families who benefit from the toy drive are required to help for at least an hour tonight. Pay it forward and all that."

"We would have helped," I say. "Why didn't you ask us to help?"

"You did help."

"How?"

"You kept me sane."

I rise onto my tiptoes and give him a quick kiss. "I'll happily keep you sane any time you need it."

Snow grins but before he can say anything, we're interrupted by Lennox.

"Can I go play with Shiloh? I see him and his mom over there." He points toward a ring toss game where the player has to get the ring on the reindeer's antlers.

"Sure, baby, go ahead." Lennox takes off running. "But stay with them at all times, okay?" I call after him.

"Okay," he yells over his shoulder.

I watch him until he's with Snow's sister and she waves at me, assuring me she's got him.

"Now what?" I turn to Snow and ask.

"Now we have fun."

Snow walks me around the carnival, introducing me to so many people that I worry I'll never remember their names. But it doesn't matter because I'll remember the stories they all share about how Snow and Satan's Legacy has helped them over the years. I'll remember the kids who tugged on his beard to make sure he really is Santa. I'll remember the stuff that matters.

"Yo, Snow!"

We both turn to see Duck running toward us.

"What's wrong?" Snow asks, shifting into MC mode quickly.

"Nothing's wrong," Duck says, out of breath when he reaches us.

"Jesus, bro, don't do that," Snow snaps. "You scared the shit out of me."

"Me too," I bitch.

"Sorry. I've been looking for you and I know we're getting close to the end of this thing. I just wanted to confirm Christmas Eve. Same time, same place?" Duck asks.

"Same as the last six years," Snow confirms. "The three of us will be there."

"The three of us will be where?" I ask, confused.

"He didn't tell you?" Duck asks. I shake my head. "Well, allow me. At ten, on Christmas Eve night, we all meet at the high school in town to load up all the gifts from the toy drive and deliver them to the houses of the families who signed up. We leave them on the porch, with a note from Santa of course, and we also make sure to leave reindeer footprints in the snow."

"Why wouldn't you tell me about that?" I ask Snow.

He glares at Duck. "Because I was hoping to surprise you and Lennox with it."

"Oh shit," Duck mumbles. "Sorry."

"It's fine," Snow says. "I don't know why I wanted it to be a surprise." He shrugs. "Just did."

"Surprise or not," I say. "I can't wait. That'll be so fun. Do all the club kids go along?"

"They sure do," Duck says. "Teaches them about giving back to the community. We absolutely want them to embrace the biker life, the fact that we're one percenters, but they also need to be good citizens and do for others. It's a lesson we've all been taught and one we vowed to keep teaching."

"Well, I, for one, am a huge fan of that lesson."

"We all—"

A cell phone rings, cutting Duck off. He and Snow both pull theirs out of their pockets and it's Snow's that's lit up with Laney's name. He taps the answer button.

"Having fun?" he asks by way of greeting. He smiles and nods, but Duck and I have no clue why because we can't hear

Laney's side of the conversation. When Snow's face darkens, he pulls the phone away from his ear and taps the speaker-phone icon. "What was that?"

"I asked if Lennox made it to you guys," she says again. "He said he was getting tired, and I saw you down the aisle of games we were in and watched him run toward you."

My head spins. Duck's eyes widen as he scans the crowd.

"When was this, Laney?" Snow asks, his tone harsh. "Because we haven't been near the games in almost an hour."

"It was about an hour ago." Her voice breaks. "I swear, Zeke, I only turned my head for a second because Shiloh fell and when I looked back, you both and Lennox were gone. I assumed he was with you."

"Well, he's not," Snow snaps. "Duck, gather everyone and fan out. Find Lennox."

Duck pulls his cell out as he rushes off to look for my son.

"Ohmigod, ohmigod, ohmigod," I cry, over and over.

"Why in the hell did you wait this long to call?" Snow barks at his sister. "It's been an hour!"

"Are you even listening?" Laney cries. "Shiloh fell. He cut his head open, so I had to take him to the EMT tent. They cleaned and bandaged him up as best they could but thought it best that I take him to the ER for stitches. They just took him back to an ER bay and I had time to call. I'm sorry!"

"Jesus," Snow mutters. "Is Shiloh gonna be okay?"

"Yeah, he'll be fine. But what about—"

"Focus on Shiloh and let me handle Lennox, okay? I'm sorry I yelled at you."

"No, no, it's my fault," she insists.

"Would you two stop arguing?!" I scream. "It's no one's fault but right now, I need you both to focus." I snatch the phone from Snow's hand. "Laney, take care of Shiloh and text us the second you're out of there so we know he's okay."

I end the call and hand the phone back to Snow. "As for

you and me, we're going to focus on Lennox because I swear to God, Zeke, if anything happens to him, I won't survive it."

Snow cups my cheeks. "Sami, we're going to find him."

"Not if we just stand here!" I yell.

I take off running, no destination in mind, and I holler Lennox's name every few seconds. Snow follows me, doing the same. By the time we've gone through the entire carnival twice, we're no closer to finding him than we were when we started.

We stop running when we reach the entrance and I double over to catch my breath, tears streaming down my face and that's when Snow's phone dings with a text. Thinking it's Laney to fill us in on Shiloh, I don't react.

"They found him," Snow says, and I straighten so fast I get dizzy. "I just got a text that says they found Lennox and he's okay. He's out at the edge of the parking lot."

"Oh thank God.

SNOW

I send a quick text to Duck and Magic, telling them to meet us at the edge of the parking lot and why, just in case we need backup. When both respond with 'on my way', I grab Sami's hand and we take off toward Lennox. What she doesn't know is who I received the text from. And I have no intention of telling her. Between Duck and I, we can handle this, but I need her as calm as possible if Lennox is going to get through this.

"I don't remember the parking lot being this big," she complains.

It isn't. I'm taking the long way around to where we need to go in the hopes that Duck and Magic will get there at the same time.

"It always seems longer when you really want to get somewhere," I say.

"I guess."

I spot Duck and Magic about ten feet from us, just beyond a row of motorcycles and wave them over. When they reach us, Sami freezes.

"What are you guys doing here?" she asks, suspicion in her tone.

They both look at me as if they have no idea how to answer so I do it for them.

"I texted them. Figured Lennox is probably scared and the more friendly faces, the better," I lie.

"Oh." She frowns. "Okay."

"This way," I say and pull her along with me, Duck and Magic following on our heels.

When we reach the edge of the lot, Sami freezes again, and this time, there is no lie that will appease her. In fact, I'm praying she doesn't kill me when this is all over.

"What the hell are you doing here?" Sami snarls.

"Mommy," Lennox cries. "I'm sorry. I didn't—"

"Shut up, brat!" Corey yells, his hand on the back of Lennox's neck.

"Majority vote coming back to bite you in the ass, huh *Pres*?" Mikey taunts from Lennox's other side.

"Corey, let him go and take me instead," Sami pleads. "You don't care about him anyway."

I know how hard those words are for Sami to say, especially with Lennox hearing all of them. I just hope he's learned exactly how much his mother loves him and how evil his father is.

"And why would I do that?" Corey asks.

"Because he's just a little boy. What can he possibly do for you?"

"Ever hear of government benefits. Brat could bring me more cash than you ever could at that filthy diner."

"Not to mention the money he can earn us through my connections," Mikey adds.

My blood runs cold. "What connections?"

"Connections Satan's Legacy could have benefited from if you weren't a bunch of pussy do-gooders. One percenter's my fucking ass."

"Mikey, you've got ten seconds to get the fuck out of

here," I snarl. "After that, I can't be held responsible for my actions."

"Seriously?" Mikey counters. "I've got the boy. What're ya gonna do?"

"You seem to be forgetting how Magic got his road name."

Mikey's eyes widen a second before a knife plunges into his forehead and he falls backward.

Sami screams, Lennox sobs, and Corey finally appears appropriately afraid.

"Let Lennox go, or your fate is gonna be the same as his," I say, nodding toward Mikey's lifeless body.

Corey pulls out a gun and points it at Lennox's head. Sami's screams intensify as she begs and pleads for her son's life. I tune it out... I have to. And I pray that Duck and Magic do the same.

"Do you really think you're quick enough to pull that trigger before one of us takes you out?" I ask.

"Uh, yeah."

"What will it take for you to let the kid go?" Duck asks, speaking for the first time.

Corey hesitates, telling me just how stupid he is. He didn't even think this plan through. He thought it would be easy for him to get into a carnival surrounded by Satan's Legacy members, take his son, and just what? Make demands and walk away like it never happened? When he doesn't even know what those demands are?

I'll give the twat this... it was easy for him to get in. He had Mikey to make that happen. I can't blame members from other chapters for not knowing about Mikey. But there will be hell to pay. Somehow, some way, they'll all know they fucked up.

Finally, Corey speaks. "I want a hundred grand and five pounds of meth."

"That's it?" I ask incredulously.

Sami stops screaming and I look at her just in time to see her face turn from scared to pure venom.

"That's all our son is worth to you?" she snarls and takes a step forward. I grab her arm, but she yanks free, her mama bear stronger than I thought.

"Duck, Magic, you see a chance, you take it," I whisper to them. "And my family better survive, or you won't."

"You got it, Pres."

I slowly walk behind Sami as she advances on Corey, keeping my hands in the air so he knows I'm not a threat.

"You didn't even want him," Sami accuses. "Remember that? Remember when you wanted me to 'get rid of it'? You never once changed a diaper, rocked him to sleep, made him soup when he was sick, went to one damn doctor's appointment. You never did anything!"

"Sami," I warn, hoping she'll stop before her actions cause irrevocable damage.

She glares at me. "Don't you dare 'Sami' me!" She resumes advancing on Corey. "He's a child, your fucking son, and all he's worth is a hundred grand and meth?"

Corey's arm shifts to point the gun at Sami and just as he swings his arm all the way in her direction...

BANG!

BANG!

Corey falls to the ground.

Lennox screams and runs toward his mom, who is swaying on her feet.

"Mommy!"

"Sami!"

When she starts to fall, I catch her and gently lower her to the ground. Her eyelids flutter and she struggles for breath.

"L-lenn-ox?" she gurgles.

"I'm right here, Mommy," Lennox cries, dropping to his knees next to her. "I'm fine."

I smack Sami's cheek. "C'mon, Angel, stay with us."

"S-so cold."

"Call a fucking ambulance!" I shout to whoever is around to listen.

"Already done," Duck says from behind me. "The others are shutting the carnival down, getting everyone else out safely."

"Zeke," Sami croaks.

"Yeah, Sami," I say, leaning close to her mouth so I can hear her. "Put pressure on her wound, Duck," I command. "I'm here, Sami."

"Take ca-are of…" Her eyes drift closed, and I smack her cheek again until she opens them. "Want you… Lenn… raise him."

"There's a lot of blood, Zeke," Duck says unnecessarily as he presses on her stomach wound.

"No shit, but she can't die," I cry. I swipe away my tears with the back of my hand. "C'mon, Sami. Don't die. We'll both take care of Lennox. We'll raise him together."

"Mommy, Snow can be my new dad," Lennox says, holding onto his mother's hand tightly.

Sami's eyes flutter. "I love… both."

And with that, her eyes close for the last time.

EPILOGUE

Snow

Christmas Eve...

"Could you possibly make this ride any bumpier?"

I stop pulling the sleigh and turn to face Sami, a giant grin on my face.

"I fail to see what's so funny," she grumbles.

"Nothing is funny," I say. "I just never thought I'd be so happy to be bitched at."

She reaches out of the sleigh and forms a snowball to launch at me but before she can, she drops it back onto the ground.

"Shit, that hurts," she complains, holding her stomach.

"You were shot a week ago and only released from the hospital yesterday," I remind her. "Of course it hurts."

"Thanks for the reminder."

"Look, I told you to stay home but you insisted on helping to deliver these presents. Be grateful that we're only doing these few blocks and I can pull you in this sleigh."

"I am grateful," she huffs. "I just hate that I'm the reason you can do this like you normally do."

"Angel, this is even better." I stop and walk to where she's sitting ensconced on blankets and kneel down in the snow. "I've got you with me." I look past her to the house behind us. "And Lennox. What more could a guy want?"

"Oh, I don't know," she says. "A girlfriend who isn't broken?"

"You're not broken," I growl. "No matter what life throws at you, you're never broken, you hear me?"

She nods. "I hear ya."

I rest my forehead against hers. "I love you, Sami. So fucking much."

"I love you, too."

"Ew, not here."

Sami and I separate, laughing at Lennox, who's now standing on the other side of the sleigh with his hands covering his eyes. Although his fingers are spread so he can still see.

"What?" I ask. "I can't tell your mom I love her?"

He lowers his arms and his face falls. "Well, yeah, I guess you can."

"Lennox, can I ask you something?"

He nods.

"You know I love you too, right?"

His eyes widen and Sami sniffles.

"You do?"

I stand and walk around to put my arms around him in a hug. "Of course I do. I couldn't love your mom and not love you."

"Okay."

"Okay?" Sami laughs. "That's it?"

"I guess you can tell her you love her any time you want," Lennox concedes like it's a very big decision he's just made.

"Thanks, son."

And when Lennox doesn't correct me, I melt inside.

I take a deep breath and clap my hands. "We've got a few more houses and then Lennox and I have a very special delivery and then it's time to sleep so Santa can come to our house."

"We have a special delivery?" Lennox asks.

"We do."

"You do?" Sami asks, quite unnecessarily.

"Yes, we do, so we need to get moving."

It takes another two hours to finish our deliveries and when I get us all back to my place, I carry Sami inside and tuck her into bed. She took a pain pill on the way home and is exhausted. Besides, I need her to be asleep while Lennox and I do our thing.

When I walk into the living room, Lennox is standing by the door.

"Let's go," he says excitedly.

"We actually don't have to go anywhere for our special delivery," I tell him. "Come sit with me on the couch?"

Lennox grumbles but he joins me on the sectional, and I can tell he's trying to keep his spirits high while being disappointed we're not going anywhere.

"This isn't exactly a delivery if we're staying home," he complains.

"Just bear with me, okay?"

"Fine."

"I have something I want to talk to you about before this *delivery*."

"Okay."

"Remember what I said when we were standing next to the sleigh?"

"Yeah." He nods. "You said you love me and Mom."

"That's right. And I wanted to ask you something about that."

"What?"

"How would you feel if I asked your mom to marry me?"

"Like be with you forever?"

"Yes, just like that."

"What about me?"

Lennox's question doesn't take me by surprise. I wish it would have because it would mean his life has been nothing but sunshine and rainbows up until this point. But let's face it, he has a great mom but even she can't make things perfect all the time. He just watched his father get shot and killed, he almost lost his mother because his father shot her, and life before that wasn't exactly stable.

"Well, see, that's my other question."

His forehead wrinkles with confusion. "Okay." He drags out the word.

"How would you feel if I were your dad?"

"Like for real, or just pretend?"

"Pretend?" I ask for clarification because I have no idea what he means by that.

"Yeah, like, would you just say I'm your kid because you have to because you'd be married to my mom?"

"Is that what you would want?"

"No," he says quickly. "I'd want you to be my real dad."

"Would you want me to adopt you?"

He shrugs. "Yeah. I mean, if we're gonna do this, we might as well do it right."

I pull him toward me in a hug, and his arms go around my neck. Tears slip down my cheeks, but I don't care. I'm so damn happy that nothing else matters. Well, nothing but getting a certain mother on board with our plan.

Lennox is the first to break the hug and when he looks at me, it's with a genuine smile.

"Now all we have to do is convince your mama," I tell him as I ruffle his hair.

"And do this special *delivery*."

Sami
Christmas Morning...

"Mom! Mom! Santa came!"

I sit in bed, sipping the coffee Snow brought me at the ass crack of dawn. I have no idea what time he came to bed, but apparently, it wasn't too late because Lennox is up, and the sun barely is.

"We better go before he barges in here," Snow says, taking my mug and setting it on the nightstand.

"Fine, if we must."

"It's Christmas morning. Where's your holiday cheer?"

"Still sleeping," I grumble as I try to swing my legs over the bed.

"Here, let me help you."

Snow walks around to my side of the bed and lifts me into his arms. He carries me out into the living room, narrowly missing banging my head on the door frame.

"I think we both need a bit more coffee," he says when he sets me on the couch.

While he does that, I glance at the tree, wrapped gifts tucked all around it. While I was in the hospital, Snow and I made a list of what I wanted to get Lennox and I see he made it happen. Based on the amount of presents, I'd say there's a lot more there than was on my list.

"Can I start, Mom?" Lennox pleads, folding his hands in front of him like he's praying. "Please, please, please?"

"Have at it, kid," Snow says before I can answer.

For the next hour, Snow and I watch Lennox tear into one gift after another. By the time he's done, he's got a pile of new clothes, several remote-control cars and motorcycles, a personalized helmet, books, and a slew of other things it would take days to list.

"I've opened all mine," Lennox announces. "Snow, it's your turn."

Lennox hands him the gift he wrapped all by himself. I have no idea what's in it because Duck took Lennox shopping, but it doesn't matter. From what I was told, Lennox picked it out himself and that's what matters.

Snow rips the paper away from the box and when he opens the lid, I can see his eyes growing shiny.

"What is it?" I ask. "Lemme see."

Snow stands from the floor and carries the box over to sit next to me. Lennox sits on my other side. Snow pulls a wooden box from the gift box and on the lid is an engraving. Snow reads the words aloud.

"What the patch binds together, let no force tear apart. Satan's Legacy now and forever."

"There's more," Lennox squeals, barely able to contain himself.

Snow reads the words in the smaller font under the club's motto. "Whether by blood or choice, we're all family."

"Lennox, that's beautiful," I tell him.

"Do you like it?" Lennox asks Snow, not caring about what I have to say.

"I love it." Snow stands and steps over my legs to lift Lennox up for a hug. "Thank you. It's perfect."

"I know," Lennox says with a laugh. "Especially now."

"Why especially now?"

"Oops," Lennox says and his face falls. "I'm sorry."

"It's okay," Snow assures him as he sets him back on the couch. "But I think it's time for us to clue your mom in on our special delivery."

"Yeah!"

"Yes, please, Mom would like to be clued in," I tell them.

"Do you think we should make her go outside for it or should we bring it in?" Snow asks Lennox.

Lennox glances at me and then back to Snow. "She looks pretty comfy. We better bring it in."

"Okay. Can you go grab it?"

"Yep."

Lennox hops off the couch and runs outside.

"What is going on?" I ask.

"You'll see," Snow assures me.

Lennox slams the door behind him and comes barreling back to the couch, jumping up next to me. In his hands are two boxes. One big and one small.

"Who should go first?" Snow asks.

"I will."

Lennox hands me the bigger box while Snow takes the smaller one and walks to my other side.

"I made that for you, Mom, last night."

I carefully take off the paper, my full attention on the gift in my hands and my son. When I expose the opening of the box, I lift it and pull out a picture frame. Immediately, tears spring to my eyes.

"You did this?" I ask Lennox, sniffling in the process.

He nods and points to the picture. "That's you and it says 'Mommy', that's me with my name, and that's Snow and it says 'Daddy'."

"This is amazing," I gush. I slowly turn toward Snow on my other side. "But—"

Snow is down on one knee, the smaller box open with a diamond ring sparkling from the center.

"Sami, Lennox and I talked last night, and we both agree that we want the three of us to be a family. A Mommy, Daddy, and son. Will you marry me?"

I look over my shoulder at Lennox and he's nodding frantically, an expectant look on his face.

"Yes, Zeke, I'll marry you."

"We'll both marry you!" Lennox shouts.

Snow slips the ring on my finger and wraps his arms around both Lennox and me. And in his little seven-year-old voice, Lennox makes the moment even more special.

"Whether by blood or choice, we're all family."

NEXT IN THE SATAN'S LEGACY MC SERIES

Toga's Demons

Toga...

Everyone has a past. It's a fact of life, one that is unavoidable. But I left mine behind eight years ago when I joined Satan's Legacy MC. I also left *her* behind. It was for the best because forbidden love doesn't even begin to cover what was starting to develop between us. Walking away from my mother was the hardest thing I've ever done, but walking away from *her* blackened my soul.

Unfortunately, time and distance doesn't mean a damn thing when she shows back up, a demon taunting me with what I can't have. Or can I? In eight years, circumstances change. What was once impossible becomes possible. And with her life in danger, I can't stay away because I'm the only one who knows her enemy, the only one who can ensure she survives to live another day.

Fallon...

I fell in love the moment I first laid eyes on *him*. Unfortunately, that was when I was sixteen and at the wedding of my father to his mother. There was something about him that called out to me, that made me believe that life would be better with him in it. Then he left and life got infinitely worse.

Fast forward eight years, and I'm in the ICU, fighting for my life because my father became even more abusive after the divorce, blaming me for all the problems in his marriage. When the man I once loved but now despise shows up, I have no choice but to spill my guts to him. Because he's the only person I have left in the world, like it or not. Will he do everything he promises and save me, give me a better life? Or will he walk away again, leaving me to pick up the pieces and likely die trying?

ABOUT THE AUTHOR

 Andi is an author of MC romance and romantic suspense who started her journey when her career in social work was no longer her passion. Her books are sassy and suspenseful with a heavy dose of sizzle and are guaranteed to deliver an HEA and all the feels. She loves writing about alpha males and the women who tame them. When she's not writing, Andi is an avid reader of the romance genre and prefers books that teeter on the edge of decent. She also loves spending time with her husband and their pack of dogs.

For access to release info, updates, and exclusive content, be sure to sign up for Andi's newsletter.

ALSO BY ANDI RHODES

Broken Rebel Brotherhood

Broken Souls

Broken Innocence

Broken Boundaries

Broken Rebel Brotherhood: Next Generation

Broken Hearts

Broken Wings

Broken Mind

Broken Loyalty

Bastards and Badges

Stark Revenge

Slade's Fall

Jett's Guard

Soulless Kings MC

Fender

Joker

Piston

Greaser

Printed in Great Britain
by Amazon